TWEEN FICTION PO

STRAIGHT PUNCH

MONIQUE POLAK

ORCA BOOK PUBLISHERS

Library and Archives Canada Cataloguing in Publication

Polak, Monique, author
Straight punch / Monique Polak.

Issued in print and electronic formats.
ISBN 978-1-4598-0391-6 (pbk.).--978-1-4598-0782-2 (bound) --
ISBN 978-1-4598-0392-3 (pdf).--ISBN 978-1-4598-0393-0 (epub)

I. Title.
PS8631.O43S77 2014   jc813'.6   C2013-906642-X
C2013-906643-8

First published in the United States, 2014
Library of Congress Control Number: 2013952980

Summary: Tessa gets caught tagging and ends up in an alternative school
where boxing is a big part of the program.

*Orca Book Publishers is dedicated to preserving the environment and has printed this book on
Forest Stewardship Council® certified paper.*

Orca Book Publishers gratefully acknowledges the support for its publishing
programs provided by the following agencies: the Government of Canada through
the Canada Book Fund and the Canada Council for the Arts, and the Province of British
Columbia through the BC Arts Council and the Book Publishing Tax Credit.

Design by Teresa Bubela and Chantal Gabriell
Cover photography by Getty Images
Author photo by Studio Iris

ORCA BOOK PUBLISHERS   ORCA BOOK PUBLISHERS
PO Box 5626, Stn. B   PO Box 468
Victoria, BC Canada   CUSTER, WA USA
V8R 6S4   98240-0468

www.orcabook.com
Printed and bound in Canada.

17 16 15 14 • 4 3 2 1

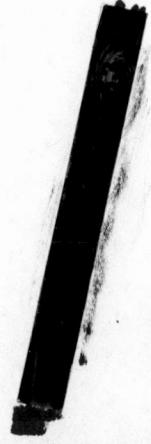

For my brother Michael, with love

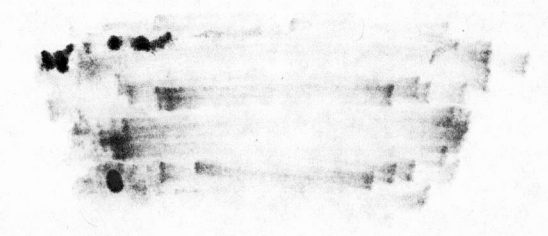

PROLOGUE

I tried to stop tagging. Okay, that isn't exactly true. I tried to stop *getting caught* tagging.

In Montreal, the cops come down hard on taggers. Especially repeat offenders like me.

The first time they caught me was two years ago. I was tagging the back wall of my school. Yeah, I know. Not too bright. Because it was my first offense, the cops waived the one-hundred-dollar fine—as long as I personally scrubbed the bricks clean.

Our principal supervised while I scrubbed. "If you ever deface school property again, Tessa McPhail"—he wagged a stubby finger in the air—"you're out. There's a waiting list of students eager to take your place at Tyndale."

Six months later, the cops caught me again. I was down by the train tracks on de Maisonneuve Boulevard. This time, I had to pay the fine. Mom thought the fear of having to dish out another hundred bucks—and possibly being sent to youth court for a third offense—would put an end to my tagging career. She was wrong.

Tagging let me feel like an artist and a rebel at the same time.

I'd go out late at night, after Mom was asleep, and watch my back. I'd wear my black hoodie and black yoga pants. If I heard a car, I'd duck into the hedges.

But one night last June, I forgot to take precautions. I'd just tagged what looked like an abandoned shed down the block from Tyndale. I left my signature tag—a black *TM*—inside a black oval. It's my ironic allusion to the trademark sign you see on almost everything you buy—cereal, bread, even cans of spray paint.

I always make my *T*s and *M*s big and bold, which is also ironic since I'm neither of those things. I'm five foot two and on the quiet side. I get more experimental with my ovals. Sometimes I turn them into wreaths, sometimes constellations. That night, I made my oval from two slivers of moon that faced each other but didn't quite touch.

I was heading home when I spotted another tagger working on a garage door on Walkley Avenue. He was perched on a wobbly wooden crate. When I got closer, I noticed his turquoise feather boa. I knew it was Pretty Boy.

We'd never met, but I'd heard of him—a flamboyant tagger with a feather-boa fetish—and I liked his work.

I looked up at his latest canvas—the garage door. The letters P and B were somewhere in there, but what knocked me out was this giant iridescent pink and turquoise butterfly with the face of an old, old man. The old, old man looked like he was about to take off on butterfly wings from the battered gray panels beneath him.

I just stood there and watched. Pretty Boy must've felt me watching, but he didn't say anything. Pretty Boy likes having an audience, though I didn't know that then.

He was adding lines to the old guy's face when the shouting started.

"That's my territory, faggot! Get the fuck outta here! Now!"

The person yelling was dressed all in black too. He was big—not just tall, but broad—with a pale face and dark flashing eyes. If I were Pretty Boy, I'd have taken off, even if it meant leaving my cans of spray paint behind. But Pretty Boy kept right on tagging. It was as if he hadn't heard a thing.

"I said now!" The voice sounded even angrier.

I still remember how my body tensed up. Fights freak me out. They have ever since the night Mom and I got caught in one of Montreal's goriest hockey riots. I can't even watch a fight on TV. If I don't turn away in time, my heart races and my palms sweat. Sometimes I actually start twitching, which is embarrassing when it happens around strangers.

That night, I could feel a fight—a big one—brewing. Pretty Boy was small and fine-boned—he'd be no match for this guy if things got physical.

I hustled into the shadows. If Pretty Boy moved quickly, he still might be able to get away. But Pretty Boy was adding another line to his old man's face.

I heard a crash as the big guy kicked over the wooden crate Pretty Boy was standing on. The crate went flying, and Pretty Boy fell to the ground. His scrawny legs made me think of that old game Pick-up Sticks.

The big guy laughed, but he wasn't done yet. He kicked Pretty Boy in the ribs, then straddled him. By then, I was twitching big-time. The big guy's eyes flashed even darker as he pressed his knee into Pretty Boy's skinny chest.

I fought the urge to turn away. I had to do something to help Pretty Boy.

"Stop it!" I yelled—or tried to yell. No sound came out. Just air.

That's when Pretty Boy looked over at me. I expected to see a look of terror in his eyes. But that wasn't what I saw.

Pretty Boy winked.

Was he out of his mind? Winking when he was about to get the beating of his life? What was he, some kind of masochist? The big guy leaned forward, breathing so heavily that the leaves on some nearby bushes rustled. He straightened, then swung his arms wildly. "Faggot!" He spat out the word.

I could see his face. Broad nose, leering mouth, sweat on his stubbly upper lip.

Pretty Boy must've seen all that too.

There was no way he was going to be able to unpin himself. Not from where he was, trapped underneath his attacker. But then Pretty Boy did something I would never have expected, not in a million years.

He threw a punch that flew up into the air, landing—*kapow*—under the big guy's jaw.

I may not have liked watching fights, but that time, I nearly yelped with pleasure.

"What the—?" the big guy said, rolling to the pavement.

When I heard the shriek of the cop car's siren, I knew I had to get out of there. The only way out was the way I'd come in—which meant I'd have to get by the big guy.

I took a deep breath as I stepped out of the shadows.

He was just getting up from the pavement. He didn't see me coming. Like he hadn't seen that punch coming from Pretty Boy. Just as I was trying to get by, he took one last wild swing at Pretty Boy and instead struck the side of my head with his fist. I fell to the ground too.

I have a vague memory—it feels more like a dream than a memory—of Pretty Boy trying to drag me away with him. "We gotta get out of here," he said, but his voice sounded like it was coming from underwater.

I also remember the sound of a can of spray paint rolling rolling rolling along the sidewalk and landing by my elbow. The big guy and Pretty Boy were gone.

The cops asked me what day it was and what city we were in. I wouldn't tell them my name though.

"You gonna tell us who whacked you in the head?" one cop asked. "Was it the same guy who tagged this garage?"

"I didn't see a thing." Talking hurt, but at least I had a voice again.

The other cop was in the cruiser, punching information into a computer. When he stepped out of the car, his hands were in his pockets. "We know who you are," he said, shaking his head. "TM. We just found a fresh tag of yours a few blocks away. You may not know this, Tessa McPhail"— I tensed up when he used my name—"but we photograph tags, and we've got yours in our system. Your photo's in there too. Looks like this is your third offense. Tonight's gonna end up costing you another hundred bucks—and quite possibly a visit to youth court. I'll bet you didn't know that shed you tagged tonight belongs to Tyndale."

My whole body went cold. Not because of the fine (though that sucked) or the threat of being sent to youth court (I'd heard from other taggers that you didn't get sent to youth court till your fourth or fifth offense). It was the principal at Tyndale I was worried about. "You're kidding," I said.

6

"Why would I kid about something like that? That shed's a storage facility. I take it you go to Tyndale—otherwise you wouldn't keep tagging in the vicinity. That principal of yours…he's one tough cookie."

The cop shook his head like he thought I was doomed. Then his eyes landed on the butterfly man. "Kind of interesting," he said. "For graffiti."

ONE

It doesn't seem fair that the school year in Montreal starts at the end of August. Not when most kids go back after Labor Day. It might have been less painful if the weather was miserable. But it was hot and the sky was robin's-egg blue. I folded down the sun visor.

My mom lifted one hand off the steering wheel and lowered her visor too. "You got yourself into this," she said.

When I didn't respond, she said it again, only louder. "I said, 'You got yourself into this.'"

I tried sinking lower in the passenger seat. You can't run away when you're in a moving vehicle. "You talking to me? I thought you were talking to the windshield."

"Very funny, Tessa."

Mom was pissed with me now, but she was the one who'd encouraged me to develop my artistic side. Even when money was tight, I had art supplies. She kept scrapbooks of every drawing I'd ever made. But I think if she'd known I was going to get into tagging—and that one day it would get me kicked out of high school—she'd have been less encouraging.

I turned on the radio. *Heavy congestion as usual on the Metropolitan eastbound. Watch out for a lane closure on Langelier Boulevard.* Even the traffic report was better than a lecture so early in the morning.

"Stay in your lane, you idiot!" Mom took one hand off the steering wheel again, this time to shake her fist at some guy in a white pickup truck. Usually Mom is like Dr. Banner—brainy and calm. Her evil Hulk only emerges on the Metropolitan Highway.

"Don't expect me to drive you every day."

"I don't."

"I'm only driving you today because it's your first day. And I might drive you now and then if the weather's bad. It's probably just as quick to take the metro—and I wouldn't have all this aggravation. I need to be at the bank at nine sharp. You nervous? You don't seem nervous."

My mom can pretty much have a conversation by herself. Maybe that's why she never remarried after an aneurysm killed my dad before I was born.

"I'd be nervous if I were you," she said.

I gave her a peck on the cheek when she pulled up in front of a narrow red-brick house. New Directions Academy was on a residential street in Montreal's north end. Montreal North is the neighborhood with the highest crime rate in the city. The Metropolitan Highway runs right through it, so even the residential streets stink of truck fumes. I'd never seen houses jammed so close together.

I thought I saw someone peer out from a crack in the curtains in the house next door, but when I looked again, the curtain was closed.

"Thanks for the lift."

When Mom smiled, I felt a little sorry for not being the kind of daughter she must have wanted. The kind who didn't get expelled from high school or have burgundy hair. I'd dyed my hair burgundy the previous summer. Cyrus loved it.

Mom ran two fingers over my cheek. "Promise me you won't get hurt, okay?"

"You worry too much."

Mom's fingers were still on my cheek. "You can't blame me for worrying, Tessa. I know how much violence upsets you. I don't think you ever really got over that…that thing."

Mom didn't like talking about the hockey riot any more than I did.

"Who knows?" I said. "Maybe this'll help. Unless, of course, it pushes me right over the edge." I made crazy eyes to demonstrate.

"That's not funny, Tessa."

I knew Mom was watching as I walked into my new school—I could hear the car idling at the curb—but I didn't look back.

The grass outside the school was brown and full of weeds. The concrete path leading to the front door was buckled and cracked. More weeds grew out from between the cracks.

I couldn't help comparing it with the lawn outside Tyndale—so green and neatly mown, it could have been AstroTurf. I'd never felt totally comfortable there, but now, looking at my new school, I was hit by a wave of nostalgia for my old one.

A guy was smoking on the creaky wooden porch. "Hey," he said. When I passed him, I smelled alcohol. Could he have been drinking this early or was the smell left over from the night before?

"Hey," I said without making eye contact.

"Welcome to Last Chance Academy," he muttered.

There were only a dozen students at New Directions Academy, all in grade ten or eleven. Last Chance would actually have been a better name for the place—everyone here had been kicked out of someplace else. Either that or they couldn't hack it in a regular school. The students here were rebels or rejects. I may never have felt like I fit in at Tyndale, but I had a feeling I'd fit in even less at this place.

It was a locked facility. The woman who buzzed me in stood up behind her desk to shake my hand.

She was tall with dark blow-dried hair and was dressed like an old-school flight attendant—in a matching tan skirt and jacket. She didn't look very old. Maybe being the receptionist here was her first job. A person has to start somewhere.

"Tessa, right?" she said, shaking my hand. "I'm Miss Lebrun. Welcome to New Directions. Did you remember your workout gear?"

I patted my backpack. "It's all here."

New Directions wasn't just an alternative school. It was an alternative to alternative schools. Half the day was for academics. The other half was for boxing.

According to the brochure I'd downloaded, the school's boxing program was supposed to build character and self-confidence. It was also supposed to channel our energy in a positive way—whatever that meant.

It wasn't my choice to go to New Directions. It was the only alternative school in Montreal with a space open in the grade-eleven class. I hadn't been sent to youth court, but the principal at Tyndale had refused to give me another chance—even when I explained that being around kids who boxed might endanger my mental health.

"Jasmine!" Miss Lebrun called out. "Jasmine!"

An Asian girl peeked out of the kitchen at the end of the hallway. Her black hair was long on one side and buzz-cut on the other. She was holding a coffee cup. Even from down the hall, I could see that her fingernails were a shiny black. "Yeah, what is it?" She sounded bored.

"Jasmine. Come meet Tessa. I want you to give her a tour of the school. Now, please."

Jasmine was dressed in skintight lime-green jeans. Her eyes were like a cat's, so light brown they were almost yellow. "Nice to meet you, Tessa," she said, though she didn't sound like she meant it.

"Okay, let's get this over with. These are the two classrooms." Jasmine pointed out two rooms off a long hallway that ran like a spine through the main floor. It was weird to see rows of desks inside a house. There were blackboards along the classroom walls and posters warning about the dangers of drugs and unprotected sex.

"What color is your hair really?" Jasmine asked me.

"Burgundy."

"Are you telling me your pubes are burgundy too?"

"I didn't mention my pubes."

"Do you always avoid answering questions?"

"Just the rude ones," I told her.

Jasmine put her hands on her hips. I could feel her sizing me up. "I've seen your type before," she said.

"What type is that?"

I figured her answer would have something to do with my hair color, but it didn't.

"You're a good girl," she said, "trying to be bad."

I didn't want to give Jasmine the satisfaction of knowing that was a pretty fair assessment.

I followed her to a narrow staircase by the kitchen. "The boxing gym's downstairs. The locker room's down there too. Do you have a lock?"

I shook my head. "I didn't think I'd need one. I thought… with only twelve students…" I was the sixth student in the grade-eleven class and there were six grade tens.

"There might only be twelve, but some of us have sticky fingers." Jasmine giggled, which made me wonder if it was her fingers she was talking about.

From halfway down the stairs, I heard a steady pounding. *Ba dum, ba dum*, then twice as fast. Someone was hitting a punching bag.

"Something wrong?" Jasmine asked when I paused on the landing. I hoped she hadn't noticed me wince.

No one's getting beaten up, I told myself. Just relax— and whatever you do, don't start twitching.

"I'm fine. Totally fine. Are the bathrooms down there too?"

"Yeah, his and hers. We're lucky there're so few girls in this dump. Just you, me and Lady Di. You'll meet her later. She's absent a lot."

The locker room had probably been a closet before New Directions moved in. The gray metal lockers looked as out of place here as the desks in the rooms upstairs. It was like seeing toilets in a kitchen.

A multicolored caterpillar was painted on the bottom of one of the lockers. Why did it seem familiar? I'd have liked to check it out, but Jasmine was tugging on my elbow. "C'mon, let's go see the gym. You'll like what's in there."

Gym smells—BO, rubber mats and musty workout gear—seeped out from under the door.

The first thing I noticed was the boxing ring—and the guy in it. He was shadowboxing—taking little steps backward and forward, throwing punches in front of him and up into the air. He was concentrating so hard, he didn't notice us. Or else he was just pretending not to notice us.

"Eye candy. And he knows it." Jasmine said it loud enough that the guy could hear her.

He smiled, but only for a second. He had a chiseled face, high forehead, straight nose, full lips. Because he wasn't wearing a shirt, I could see he was ripped. His chest muscles rippled with every punch. Eye candy was right.

"Hey, Jabbin' Jasmine," a voice called out.

"Hey, Coach." Jasmine's face looked different when she smiled. Softer.

The coach was sitting in a green plastic lawn chair by the back of the ring. "Gonna introduce me to your pal?"

"She's not my pal. She's the new student. Tessa something or other."

The coach laughed. He obviously appreciated Jasmine's sense of humor more than I did. "Good to meet you, Tessa Something-or-Other. I'm Big Ron. You ready to start your boxing career?" he asked without getting up from his chair.

"Uh-huh." Did I sound as nervous as I felt?

I followed Jasmine over to where Big Ron was sitting. He wasn't called Big Ron for nothing. The guy was the size of two regular Rons. I tried not to stare when he stood up to shake my hand. He waddled over, his face red from the exertion. This was our boxing coach?

"I'm lookin' forward to working with you," Big Ron said, and I managed to mutter something about looking forward to working with him too.

Big Ron turned to the guy in the ring. "Nice work on your combinations this morning, Randy Randy." Randy Randy? It wasn't hard to figure out how this guy earned his nickname. "Just make sure you keep your chin down. And don't forget to say hello to Tessa Something-or-Other."

Randy licked the sweat off his upper lip. "Hi," he said. "How 'bout we"—he paused—"we shake hands when I'm not all sweaty?"

"Sure." My voice came out higher than usual. I was sure he'd seen me admiring his pecs.

"I gotta shower," Randy said. "Miss Lebrun"—he paused again—"she gets pissed if we're late."

"Miss Lebrun?" Did the secretary take attendance at New Directions?

"Yeah," said Jasmine. "You met her upstairs. She's pretty strict about attendance and stuff, but don't worry. Miss Lebrun's okay."

So, I thought, my new teacher looks like she's in her early twenties, and my boxing coach is so fat he can hardly move. What could be next?

Next came when I followed Jasmine back upstairs and into the grade-eleven classroom.

Miss Lebrun, who was standing by the blackboard, gestured for me to take a seat at the front.

The boy slumped in the desk next to mine had his head turned away from me, so I couldn't see his face.

But I recognized the turquoise boa.

What was Pretty Boy doing here?

TWO

Miss Lebrun eyed the clock over the classroom door. "It's eight fifteen—time to get started. For those of you who were with me last year, welcome back. It's nice to see you. I hope you didn't get into too much trouble over the summer."

Jasmine and a couple of other students sitting at the back snickered.

Pretty Boy turned his head so that he was facing me. His eyebrows (one of them was pierced) lifted in surprise when he saw me. "You!" he said, mouthing the word so Miss Lebrun wouldn't hear.

"I also want to welcome a new student, Tessa McPhail." Miss Lebrun turned to me. "Tessa, it's good to have you with us. We hope our school will be a great experience for you, that it'll take you in new—"

Miss Lebrun paused—for effect, I figured—and Pretty Boy finished her sentence. "Directions," he muttered. He reminded me of the dormouse in *Alice's Adventures in Wonderland*. He'd probably been up late tagging. I remembered his drawing of the butterfly with the old man's face.

The multicolored caterpillar I'd noticed on one of the lockers downstairs made sense now. It was Pretty Boy's.

"That's right, Percy. New directions. Like all of you, Tessa is here because she's journeying in a new direction."

My face got hot as I felt six pairs of eyes on me, sizing me up. They were trying to figure out what *journey* had landed me here. I knew that because I was wondering the same thing about them.

"Let's start with a quick review of the basic rules. Percy, I'm not interrupting your morning nap, am I?"

Without lifting his head from his desk, Pretty Boy met Miss Lebrun's eyes. "I haven't missed a word you said, Miss L. But can't you call me Pretty Boy this year?"

"It says Percy on this list from the Ministry of Education," Miss Lebrun said, waving her attendance sheet in the air. "So that's the name we'll be using in this classroom."

Pretty Boy sighed. I felt bad for him. Imagine getting saddled with a name like Percy.

"We call him a lot of names besides Percy," the guy who'd been smoking on the porch called from the back of the room. He had a raspy voice.

"I'm sure you do, William. All right, then, let's talk about rules. As most of you already know, punctuality matters at New Directions. I expect you to get to class on time and I expect your assignments to be turned in on time too. No bathroom breaks during class except in case of emergency, phones off, no texting, nothing of that sort. Most of all, I expect all of you to be respectful, to me and to one another." Miss Lebrun looked around the classroom, her gaze falling on each of us individually. "I have a sheet for attendance, a sheet for grades and another sheet for recording any cases of misbehavior. If you misbehave more than twice, you know the consequences."

"No training for a week," said a deep voice at the back of the classroom.

I hadn't heard Randy come in. His soapy smell traveled to the front of the room.

"That's right, Randall."

I didn't say what I was thinking—so what if I don't get to train for a week?

For me, that would be a reward, not a punishment.

Miss Lebrun made each of us say our name. I knew she did the exercise for my benefit, since the others already knew each other. Don't make us say what brought us here, I prayed, and she didn't.

I really hoped New Directions wasn't going to be some sort of group therapy for troubled teens.

Miss Lebrun reached into a cardboard box beside her desk and took out a stack of notebooks. They were the kind you get at the dollar store, with black speckled covers. "Say hello to your new journal," she said as she walked to the back of the classroom and began handing them out.

A couple of students groaned.

"This journal thing must be her latest experiment," Pretty Boy whispered to me. "Consider yourself a guinea pig."

Miss Lebrun smiled when she handed me my journal. Then she went back to her desk. "I took a great online course this summer about journaling," she said—and when I turned to look at Pretty Boy, he whispered, "Told you so"— "and so this year, I've decided we'll begin every morning with journal time. Sometimes we'll do what's called *free writing*. Other times, like today, I'll assign a subject. I have two subjects for you today. First, I want you to write a greeting to your journal."

"You gotta be kidding," Jasmine said.

"Let's get this straight—you want us to *greet* a book?" William asked.

"I'm not kidding. I just want you to take a few minutes to say hello to your journal. After all, the two of you are going to be spending a lot of time together this year."

Miss Lebrun took a black speckled notebook for herself too. She sat at her desk, writing her own greeting.

I wondered what she was writing—*Lord, give me strength to deal with this gang of delinquents?*

I didn't know what to write. As I was thinking that, Miss Lebrun looked up from her notebook and said, "It doesn't matter what you write as long as it's honest. By the way," she added, "I should have explained that you won't have to share what you write in your journal with me or with the class. Unless, of course, you'd like to."

That helped. I picked up my pen and started writing.

Greetings, speckled notebook. I can't think of anything else to say. Well, okay, here's one thing. I really don't feel like I belong here with these kids. And here's another: I just want to get this school year over with. And here's another: I really hope I don't get the shit beaten out of me by one of these demented boxers.

I figured swearing was allowed if I was the only one who'd be reading my journal.

When I ran out of ideas, I looked over at Pretty Boy. He must have felt me watching him because he slid his notebook over to the edge of his desk so I could see it. Only he hadn't written a single word. Instead, he was making a drawing. A drawing of me—with butterfly wings. The drawing freaked me out. It isn't every day a person sees herself with wings sprouting from her shoulders. But I had to admit, he'd gotten my expression right. Pretty Boy's butterfly girl looked lost and confused, as if she couldn't decide if she was a butterfly or a girl.

Miss Lebrun wanted us to try one more exercise before starting math. "William, do you mind lending me your baseball cap?"

"You need my baseball cap for a writing exercise, Miss? Is that something you learned online too?" William asked, but he had already whipped off his cap and was bringing it over to Miss Lebrun.

Pretty Boy looked up from the drawing he was still working on. "You gonna pull a rabbit out of that sweaty cap?" he asked.

Miss Lebrun dropped some folded-up bits of paper into the cap. "We are going to pull something out of William's cap. Only it's not a rabbit." Then she circulated between the desks and we each had to take one of the folded-up bits. Mine had the number eleven on it.

"I'm really excited about this exercise. We'll begin with our journals closed," Miss Lebrun said, which surprised me. "Eyes closed too." Which surprised me even more. Whoever heard of writing with your eyes closed?

"Take a couple of deep breaths in and out. Like this." She demonstrated. I didn't close my eyes right away. But Miss Lebrun's eyes were shut, making her look even younger. A couple of students at the back giggled, but I could hear the others breathing in and out, so I did too, even if it seemed like the weirdest writing exercise. Ever.

Miss Lebrun's voice was softer now. She didn't sound like the Miss Lebrun who just minutes before had been waving her Ministry of Education attendance sheet at us. "Writers commonly draw on their own memories for inspiration. This exercise we're about to do is meant to help us retrieve an old memory so we'll be able to write about it. We each chose a number from the cap and we're going to write about a memory associated with that age. I need to warn you, this exercise can have a powerful effect. Only go as deep into the memory as you're comfortable going. If it gets to be too much for you, you can stop at any point. All right then, let's begin. I want all of you to try and remember what it felt like to be the age that's on your slip of paper."

Of all the numbers I could have picked from that baseball cap, why did I have to choose eleven?

"Let your mind land on some memory from when you were that age, a memory…" Miss Lebrun continued.

I wondered if she was trying to hypnotize us, repeating the word *memory* like that.

"Any memory that comes to you will do. Just let the memory land. Don't fight it."

Fight it? Did she have to say that? If there was one thing in my life I wanted to forget, it was the fight I'd witnessed when I was eleven. It was April 2008—the night of the Montreal Canadiens' seventh-game win over the Boston Bruins. Who would have guessed that a party—a giant party with thousands of fans celebrating that their team had advanced in the playoffs—would turn violent?

Miss Lebrun was speaking again. "Look around in your memory. What do you see? Is it bright or dark? Are you alone or are there others with you?"

I tried remembering something else. I tried remembering my eleventh birthday—the cake with pink frosting, me blowing out the candles while my friends clapped and Mom snapped pictures.

But my mind wouldn't let me land there. It was taking me back to the riot. I was the one who'd talked Mom into going for dinner at our favorite chicken-and-ribs place downtown. "I don't know, Tessa. There's a big game tonight—we might have trouble parking."

Parking turned out to be the least of our problems.

Is it bright or dark? It was both. Dark by the time we left the restaurant. Bright because of the fires.

I could still see the orange flames.

The streets were thick with people celebrating—laughing, cheering, tipping beer into their mouths. Whose idea was it to set fire to a police car? And then, like the orange flames, the idea spread.

Are there other people with you? There was Mom, but mostly there was the mob. More people than I'd ever seen all at once, shoving in every direction. Some wanting to get closer to the burning cars, some to the storefronts on Ste-Catherine Street, where they were smashing windows, helping themselves to whatever was inside. Some wanting to get away or, like me and Mom, back to their cars.

"Add sound," Miss Lebrun's voice urged. "What sounds do you hear? Someone laughing or maybe someone crying—or shouting?"

Shouting, yes, over the shattered glass. Angry, drunken shouting coming closer.

"Go back to Boston, you asshole!" In my memory, I heard a man's voice slurring his words. Then someone shouting back, "Leave me alone! I got the right to root for my team!"

Then my mom's voice. "Whatever you do, Tessa," she was saying, "don't let go of my hand." It was the first time I'd ever heard her sound afraid. Which scared the shit out of me.

"Add touch," Miss Lebrun told us. "Reach back into your memory and touch something—what does it feel like?"

I thought about making myself stop, the way Miss Lebrun had said we could, but the memory was begging to be remembered.

Two men were punching each other. People tried to get out of their way, but there was no room. I felt my mother squeezing my hand…but then I couldn't feel her anymore. More punching—louder, harder. I wanted to cry out, tell them to stop, but my voice didn't work. I wanted to move, even just an inch, but my legs didn't work either.

"Stop it!" other people called from the crowd.

The two guys didn't stop. More punches, then screaming.

One man fell, crashing into me and knocking me down to the pavement. As if that wasn't bad enough, he tripped, landing on top of me. He must have weighed two hundred pounds. I could hardly breathe. I was drowning in a sea of feet and legs.

"What do you feel?" Miss Lebrun asked. "The rough bark of a tree trunk or perhaps someone's hand, soft and powdery?"

Mom's hand. Where was she? I tried feeling for her fingers, but all I felt was the man's weight—and then the rough sole of someone's boot pressing down on my hand.

The mob was a monster. The only part of me that wasn't trapped underneath the man was my elbow. I tried to use it to push the man away, but it was no use. Was he dead?

"A kid's getting trampled!" someone yelled.

No one heard—or if they did, they paid no attention.

"Tessa!" My mom's voice. Then, "Please! Help me find my daughter!" Mom's voice was coming closer. Somehow, I managed to turn my head so I could see a little.

Mom was elbowing her way toward me. She'd seen me too. "My daughter's under there!" Her voice was hoarse.

"What do you think you're doing, shoving me like that?" a man called out.

Sounds of a scuffle. Then a woman—*Don't let it be Mom*—crying out in pain. The crunch of glass somewhere nearby. I moved my hands closer to my sides. If it was a beer bottle that had broken, I didn't want to get cut. But it wasn't a beer bottle. It was a pair of wire-rimmed glasses. One lens was cracked down the middle; the other was in shards.

Those were my mom's glasses. She was practically blind without them. But now she was on the ground too, trying to pull me out from underneath the drunk man. I gasped when I saw her face. A jagged gash under one eye. Blood dripping down her face, over her lips, onto her chin.

"It's okay, Tessa," she kept saying. "Everything's going to be okay."

I knew it wasn't true. How could it be when she was bleeding like that? And I knew something else too—it was my fault. I should never have let go of her hand.

Miss Lebrun was speaking again. "Let's add smell next. Of all the senses, smell is the most powerful trigger of memory. What does your memory smell like? If you can, follow the smell deeper into your memory."

I coughed. The metallic smell of blood was in my nose, stuck in the little hairs inside.

"Let's open our notebooks now," Miss Lebrun was saying. "We're going to write down all the details that came back to us. For once, I don't want you to worry about making proper sentences. Just get the details down."

That was when I heard a loud crash. Someone had thrown a desk against the wall.

Jasmine.

She was rushing out of the classroom.

"Jasmine? Come back! Jasmine!" Miss Lebrun called after her.

Jasmine was already out the front door of the school. Through the window, I saw her flying down the street, her black hair flapping against one side of her face.

THREE

By the end of our first break, Jasmine had come back.

Pretty Boy had predicted it. "It isn't like she has anyone to go to," he told me when Miss Lebrun went to the front porch to call after Jasmine. "She's an orphan."

"An orphan? You're kidding." I'd only read about orphans. Anne of Green Gables, Harry Potter and the Baudelaire siblings were all orphans. I'd never met one in real life.

"Yup," Pretty Boy said. "Both her parents died in a car wreck. She was fourteen when it happened. I bet Miss Lebrun wishes she'd left that particular number out of the cap."

"So who does Jasmine live with?"

"Her aunt Melinda. But let's just say Aunt Melinda isn't exactly a model citizen. Even by my standards, which are admittedly low."

I felt guilty for ever thinking I had it rough, being raised by just my mom—especially since mine was, as she liked to remind me, the sort of mom who counted as two parents.

We could stay in during the breaks between classes or hang out in the little yard behind the house. I opted for out. The word *yard* was an exaggeration. It was a rectangle of grass in sorrier condition than the grass in front of the school. There was a rusted-out basketball hoop on an even rustier stand.

The only pretty thing about the yard was the bed of giant sunflowers on the other side of the chain-link fence separating school property from the house next door. The flowers' hairy stalks were as thick as kitchen pipes. They leaned in toward the fence as if curious to know what was going on at New Directions.

Randy and Pretty Boy were shooting hoops. Pretty Boy's turquoise feather boa dragged on the ground when he dribbled. William was there too. Except for Miss Lebrun, everybody called him Whisky, for obvious reasons. He was sitting on the stoop next to Jasmine. Her eyes were red and puffy.

"Everything all right?" I asked her.

"Allergies," she said, but I knew she was lying.

Randy's phone rang, but he didn't bother answering it.

"What if it's one of your lady friends looking for a little company?" Pretty Boy said with a grin.

Randy jumped into the air and slid the ball into the hoop before he answered. "She can always leave a message," he said.

Pretty Boy had the ball now. "That's your secret, isn't it? Ignore 'em—and they come back for more."

A woman next door was hanging out laundry. Her frizzy brown hair made her look like a walking dandelion. She was arranging everything on her clothesline by size. At the far end were towels and jeans, then T-shirts, the clothes pegs under the armpits. Now she was hanging socks, each one with its matched partner. White gym socks last. I wondered if, when she took the clothes off the line, they smelled of car and truck exhaust.

Pretty Boy made a basket and celebrated by doing a chicken dance, flapping his arms and clucking loudly. We laughed, but the woman next door shook her head, and Pretty Boy gave her the finger. "Too bad they don't teach you manners in there," the woman said as she took her laundry basket and retreated into her house.

Jasmine rolled her eyes. "What's your problem, Pretty Boy?"

Pretty Boy threw another hoop. "Anger management," he said, without lifting his eyes from the basketball. "What's yours?"

When we got back from our break, a middle-aged bald guy was sitting on Miss Lebrun's desk, spinning his thumbs in a way that made me wonder if he had ADD.

"Who's he?" I whispered to Pretty Boy.

"That's Mr. Turner, the principal. Not to worry though— he doesn't come around much." Pretty Boy explained that

Mr. Turner was also the principal of a school for kids with disabilities and an adult-ed facility in the city's west end. "It's the new economy," he said. "One man, three jobs."

I noticed that Mr. Turner's forehead was furrowed with lines, undoubtedly caused by years of dealing with difficult students.

Miss Lebrun had rounded up the grade tens too. Because there weren't enough desks for all of us, they had to sit on the windowsills.

"I came by to wish you all a good year," Mr. Turner said after Miss Lebrun signaled him that we were all there. "I also want to show my support for Miss Lebrun. You're lucky to have a teacher as engaged and committed as she is."

"You're engaged, Miss L? How come you didn't tell us?" Whisky called out.

Miss Lebrun blushed.

"By engaged," Mr. Turner said, "I mean enthusiastic. I'm expecting you to give Miss Lebrun your full coopera-tion. I don't have to remind you that if any of you don't make it here at New Directions…well, you won't have too many other options. And as I'm sure you know, your lives are going to be a lot more difficult without that high school leaving certificate. We want to help you—but you're also going to need to help yourselves…and each other."

Under his desk, Pretty Boy's fingers were opening and closing like a duck's beak. I gathered he didn't have a high opinion of Mr. Turner.

"There's something else I need to discuss with you. When I arrived at New Directions today, the phone rang and I took the call. It was one of our neighbors, and she wasn't too happy." Mr. Turner looked at his shoes—they were brown and scuffed. Maybe men with three jobs didn't have time to polish their shoes.

He looked back up at us. "I'm going to be straight with you. This neighbor isn't too pleased about having us next door." Something about the way Mr. Turner used the word *us* sounded phony. I had a feeling the neighbor didn't mind having Mr. Turner next door. It was the dozen juvenile delinquents she was worried about.

Then came the kicker.

"What she's most upset about is that you're learning to box."

Randy groaned. Jasmine shook her head. Whisky burped. Even Pretty Boy lifted his head off his desk and said, "What the fuck?" Then, before Miss Lebrun or Mr. Turner could reprimand him, he put his hand over his mouth and did it for them. "Language, Percy!"

Mr. Turner gave us a tight smile. "I assured this woman that none of you pose a threat to her safety or the safety of this community, but let's just say she wasn't convinced. She's talking about starting a petition." He looked down at his shoes, then up again. "She wants the school board to close down New Directions. Miss Lebrun and I debated whether I should tell you this, but in the end we decided it was best to

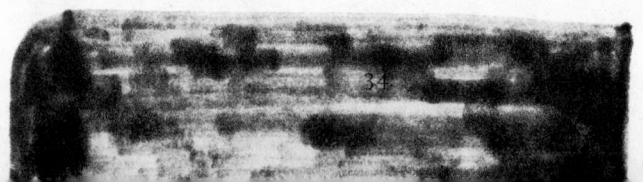

make you aware of the situation. Now, of course, you'll under-stand why it's absolutely essential for you to be on your very best behavior—not just inside this school, but outside too." Mr. Turner looked around the classroom. "Are you reading me?"

"We're reading you, sir," Whisky called out. "Best behavior—inside and out." If Whisky hadn't belched at just that moment, I might have thought he meant it.

After Mr. Turner left, we did math exercises. Miss Lebrun walked between the desks, supervising. "This is math, Percy," she said, tapping Pretty Boy's desk. "Not art class." When she eyed the row of calculations in my notebook, she nodded. "Randall," I heard her say when she got to the back of the room, "do you want me to look over your answers with you now or should we wait until later?"

When Miss Lebrun wasn't looking, Percy checked the time on his phone—twice. And when I looked to the back of the room where Jasmine was sitting, she was punching the air in front of her.

At Tyndale, there'd been kids (not that I was ever one of them) who liked math. At New Directions, math seemed to mean only one thing—it was the last class before boxing.

When I walked into the gym, somebody barked.

At first, I thought maybe one of the guys was teasing me. Not a very nice way to greet a new student.

I didn't expect to see a brindled pit bull lying on his stomach at the side of the room. "Yikes," I said, taking a step back. "What's he doing here?"

"You allergic?" a girl called out. She had bleached-blond hair and eyes rimmed with thick black liner. She was wearing a loose-fitting peasant blouse, faded jeans and a pair of seriously cool silver cowboy boots.

"No. But aren't pit bulls...you know...dangerous?"

The girl laughed. "Ruger? Dangerous? No way. This dog's a pussycat. Come over and say hi to him. I'm Di, though Big Ron likes to call me Lady Di. Not that I'm much of a princess. Wanna cracker?" She extended her arm so slowly it felt like slow motion and offered me a box of soda crackers.

Ruger wagged his long whiplike tail. "Why'd you name him Ruger?" I asked.

Di scratched the dog behind his ears. She did that slowly too, and Ruger wagged his tail some more. "A Ruger's a gun. My brother got shot two years ago. The gun that killed him was a Ruger."

I knew from the way Di was watching my face that she wanted to shock me, so I tried not to react. I just nodded like I was used to meeting kids whose siblings had been murdered. But afterward, when we were in the girls' locker room, changing into our workout clothes, I told Di I was sorry about her brother. "I don't get why you named your dog after the gun that killed him though. Isn't that the sort of thing you'd want to forget?"

"Not me." Di tapped her chest. "I'm into remembering. Even the rough stuff. Especially the rough stuff."

Big Ron started us off with half an hour of warm-ups. Everything from calf raises to lunges, followed by stretching. The guy was a drill sergeant. He also wasn't too good with numbers. "Forty jumping jacks!" he bellowed.

I knew I'd done forty because I was counting them in my head, hoping to get them over with ASAP, but when I stopped, Big Ron glared at me and told me I still had ten left to do.

"But I counted them!" I protested. I wiped the sweat from my forehead—some of it dripped and made my eyes burn.

"Who's the coach here—me or you?"

I figured it was easier to keep jumping than to argue with Big Ron. But man, those jumping jacks—especially the extra ten—were torture. Even the backs of my knees were sweating. There were a couple of ceiling fans in the gym, but all they did was stir around the hot air.

"How come he doesn't open the windows?" I asked Di when Big Ron wasn't looking.

"The neighbors," she said. "The sound of punching bothers them."

I didn't tell her I knew how they felt.

"You'll need these." After our warm-up, Big Ron tossed me a pair of rolled-up black hand wraps. "You owe me six bucks for those, Tessa Something-or-Other. Don't forget to pay me back. No interest if it's within a week."

"Thanks," I said as I tore off the packaging and began unrolling the wraps. They were longer than I'd expected, with Velcro fasteners at both ends.

The others were putting on their own hand wraps, winding them over their wrists, then across their knuckles. Though it seemed complicated to me, they made it look easy.

"No rings!" Big Ron said when he spotted the ring on my middle finger. It was a thin gold band shaped like a curved paintbrush. When Cyrus had given it to me for my birthday, he'd shown me the stamp that said *14 karat gold* inside. I loved that ring, even if a spray can would have been more my style than a paintbrush.

"Even with boxing gloves on, you could cut yourself pretty bad or injure your opponent," Big Ron said, "if you box with a ring on."

Not wearing the ring made me feel strange. I didn't even take it off to shower or when I went to sleep. It had started to feel like part of me. Because I didn't know where else to leave it, I put it on the floor by Big Ron's chair. That way, I'd be able to keep an eye on it during the lesson.

I tried putting on my wraps, but I got them tangled up, and I hadn't made them as tight as I needed to.

"Let me help you," Big Ron offered.

He still hadn't gotten out of his chair. I'd have liked to see *him* do fifty jumping jacks.

I let him put on the wraps for me. "Now, watch how I do it," he said. "First, you got to spread your fingers apart.

Then you wrap your wrist a few times. Like this. Nice and snug." Big Ron's hands were as big as bear paws. I watched how he wrapped my right hand, then my left. Wrist, knuckles, thumb, then back to my wrist and knuckles. How would I ever remember all that?

Except for Pretty Boy, who was working on his focus by hitting the speed ball, the others were working in pairs. I'd never heard so much grunting and groaning. Randy and Whisky were shadowboxing at opposite ends of the ring, and Di and Jasmine were alternating on the punching bag. I could see that Di took her time with things, setting herself up in front of the bag and pausing between punches. Jasmine was a speed demon. It wasn't hard to tell why Ron called her Jabbin' Jasmine—she threw one quick punch after another without breaking a sweat.

Big Ron was still in his chair. "The first thing you need to learn," he told me, "is proper fighting stance. In boxing, proper fighting stance is like the trunk of a tree. Without the trunk, you got nothing." He made a zero with his fingers.

Then he got up from his lawn chair and waddled over to demonstrate.

I didn't want Big Ron to catch me staring at him, so I looked away. That's when my eyes landed on some photographs mounted over the wall of mirrors in front of me. Some of the photos were black-and-white, so I figured they'd been taken a long time ago. They were photos of boxers—all of them men. How come, I wondered, there were no women on Big Ron's wall?

It took me a moment to realize that one of the buff young boxers in the photos was Big Ron before he got big. I recognized the eyes, the crooked smile and the square jawline. The photo must have been taken after a bout, because Big Ron was holding a trophy, his face sweaty.

I'd been wondering what misadventures had brought the other students to New Directions, but now I wondered about Big Ron too. He must've dreamed of bigger, better things than coaching boxing at a school for troubled teens.

"I see you're admiring my wall of fame," Big Ron said.

"That's you, isn't it?"

"Yup," Big Ron said, without looking at the photo. "In my glory days. Now let's work on your fighting stance. You gotta angle your body so you're facing your opponent sideways. Your left foot's in front of you at one o'clock. Right foot's back at two o'clock. Like this." When Big Ron demonstrated the move, I could picture him for a moment as a fit young boxer. But then the moment passed and Big Ron was back in front of me, his giant belly bulging like a truck tire over his sweatpants.

Big Ron studied my feet. "Move your left foot a little to the inside. Now you got it. Okay, clasp your hands behind your back and rotate your hips from side to side."

I did that for a while. Big Ron went back to his chair. "You're building muscle memory," he told me. "Your body's learning what proper fighting stance feels like."

Every couple of minutes, he'd bark instructions to the others. "Move your hands more quickly," he told Pretty Boy. "Not so Schwarzenegger-ish," he said to Di. "Not so fast," he told Jasmine. When Whisky had a coughing fit, Big Ron called out, "If you cough like that during a fight, you'll go down. You're gonna knock yourself out with your own bad habits, son."

Big Ron sighed and looked back at me. Then he got up from his chair again. I got the feeling he wished he didn't have to. "All right, Tessa Something-or-Other, what do you say I teach you how to throw a straight punch?"

Something in my stomach clenched. I had never thrown a punch in all my life. I took a deep breath. This wasn't going to be easy. But if I wanted to graduate from high school, I'd have to do it. "I say okay."

"You gotta remember to breathe from your belly and keep your chin down. You're gonna release your arm straight out like this." Big Ron demonstrated. "Okay, try it."

I could feel my heart rate quicken and the little hairs on my arms stand up. It was as if every ounce of me was opposed to what I was about to do. I'd seen how quickly people lost control, how ugly things could get and how violence could affect innocent bystanders. Mom and I had been innocent bystanders.

But I did want to graduate from high school.

So I took another deep breath and released my arm the way Big Ron had shown me.

41

"No, no, no," he said, shaking his head. Then he stepped right in front of me, so close I could smell his mouthwash. I fought the urge to step away.

"Show me again," he said.

I extended my jabbing arm.

That was when Big Ron's giant paw came straight at me, whistling through the air. I was so scared, I shut my eyes.

"Eyes open!" Big Ron bellowed. At just that moment, his punch grazed the middle of my jaw. He hadn't struck me hard, but still, it had stung, and my whole body was shaking. I wanted to step back, but I couldn't move. There it was again—that frozen feeling. Trapped, the way I'd been underneath that drunk the night of the riot.

I rubbed the spot on my chin where Big Ron had hit me. "Hey," I managed to say. "That hurt."

I thought Big Ron might apologize, but all he did was laugh. "That didn't hurt you," he said. "It took you by surprise."

I wondered if he could be right. Maybe I was more surprised than hurt. Still, it wasn't nice of him. Not on my first day of boxing lessons. "Why'd you do that?" I asked him.

Big Ron grinned. "I figured it'd help you learn to keep your chin down the way I told you to. And you didn't rotate your hips either. Let's try it again, paying attention to my instructions this time, Tessa Something-or-Other."

I didn't like being called Tessa Something-or-Other, but I decided this wasn't the right time to complain. I had bigger things to worry about—like Big Ron's paw. So I took another deep breath and got back into fighting stance. This time, I kept my chin down.

"That's my girl!" Big Ron said when I finally got the move right.

I couldn't help liking how he'd called me *his girl*. But when I thought about how Big Ron had nearly whacked me in the face, I decided I'd never feel comfortable in this boxing gym or at this school. The sounds of the other kids groaning and whacking the punching bags would always make me jump. Sending someone like me to a school that had a boxing program was like forcing someone who got airsick to become a pilot.

That's what I was thinking when my eyes scanned the floor next to Big Ron's chair.

My ring. It was gone.

FOUR

I wish now I hadn't freaked out. But I did. Big time.

"My ring!" I shouted—so loudly that everyone in the gym froze. Randy's arms fell limp by his sides. Jasmine dropped her punch in midair. Di just stared at me. Big Ron stood in front of me like some gigantic statue. Even Ruger lifted his head and looked up at me with sad, worried eyes.

"It was right there," I said, rushing over to Big Ron's lawn chair and pointing to the spot on the cement floor where I'd left Cyrus's ring. I dropped to my knees and ran my fingers along the floor, feeling for the ring. "I know I left it here!" I wailed. "And now it's gone!"

Big Ron walked over to his chair. The others still didn't move. Maybe they hadn't expected me to be a shrieker. I suppose I looked like the sort of person who could control herself—and usually, I was. But now that I'd started shrieking, I couldn't stop. "My boyfriend gave it to me. And now it's gone! It was right here!"

Big Ron laid his paw on my shoulder. "Get a grip, Tessa," he said sternly. "Freaking out isn't going to help you find your ring."

I shook his hand loose. "Don't tell me to get a grip," I hissed. "I want my ring back!"

Jasmine came over now too. "Let me help you look," she offered, squatting down to help me check the floor around Ron's chair.

"It's not there," I told her. "I looked already. It's gone. And I want it back!"

Jasmine backed away. I suppose I should have been grateful she wanted to help, but I couldn't help wondering if maybe *she* had taken my ring. Hadn't she warned me that some of the students here had *sticky fingers*?

"Did you take it?" I asked her, my voice louder than I wanted it to be.

Jasmine looked at me as if I'd punched her. "Why would I take your dumbass ring?"

"I don't know why. And it's not a dumbass ring." That's when I started to sob—big sorry-for-myself sobs that made my shoulders shake. I don't think I was sobbing just about the ring. Maybe I was sobbing about other stuff too—like getting myself expelled from Tyndale, being forced to go to New Directions, messing up, disappointing my mom.

Jasmine got up and shook her head. Then she stomped back to the punching bag and gave it a huge whack. The bag absorbed her punch and then swung in the air like a giant leather pendulum.

Pretty Boy was stretching by the windows. He didn't come over—maybe I'd scared him with my shrieking—but he called out from where he was, "Your ring was shaped like a paintbrush, right?"

The way he used the word *was*—as if I'd never see Cyrus's ring again—got me even more upset. And now the angry feelings came back like a giant wave, the kind you can't escape when it's rolling in your direction.

I stood up and said, "One of you stole my ring." My voice was lower now, but colder than ice. "You'd better give it back to me. Or I'll...I'll..."

"What're you going to do exactly?" Di asked.

Our eyes met. I knew that inside she was laughing at me, enjoying how upset I was.

"I'll call the police," I said. It was all I could think of.

Now someone in the gym did laugh. I wasn't sure who.

Big Ron came to stand next to me. This time, he didn't try putting his hand on my shoulder. "I hate to tell you this, but the police don't take complaints from this school—or its students—too seriously," he said.

Then Big Ron put his hands on his hips and cleared his throat. "I don't care who took Tessa's ring. But I'll tell you one thing and one thing only—by tomorrow morning at eight AM and not a second later, I expect to see that ring back on the floor by this here chair. Now quit your lollygagging and get back to work!"

Big Ron pointed one fat finger at Jasmine. "I'm going to watch what's going on in the boxing ring. I want you to work with Tessa on her rotations, and when you're done with that, you can watch her throw a few straight punches."

I knew Big Ron had paired us up because of the way we'd talked to each other before. He didn't notice Jasmine sneer as she walked over, swishing her hips like some exotic dancer.

I pretended not to notice either. I was thinking about my ring and wondering if it would be back on my finger by tomorrow morning at eight AM. I could almost feel it there. I was thinking, too, how Big Ron had stopped calling me Tessa Something-or-Other. To be honest, I kind of missed it.

I got into my fighting stance. Left foot at one o'clock, right foot at two o'clock. There, I thought, not bad. Then I clasped my hands behind my back and started rotating my hips the way Big Ron had shown me.

Jasmine watched without saying a word. If she'd taken my ring, where had she put it? Her workout shorts had no pockets. Maybe she'd tucked it inside her gym bra.

I knew I had to concentrate on my moves. For now, there was nothing I could do about my ring. Big Ron knew these kids better than I did. Maybe his plan would work. He'd certainly defused the tension in the room. And now, as I felt my weight shift from one side of my body to the other, I was sorry I'd lost it the way I had. The other kids had seen a side of me I'd rather not have shared with them, especially not on my first day at New Directions.

Randy was getting a sip of water from the fountain at the front of the gym. His shoulders glistened with sweat. I could hear Ruger panting. Randy walked over and reached down for the dog's water bowl. "You thirsty? Is that what you're trying to say, Ruger?"

Ruger thumped his tail. Randy filled the bowl. When he walked back to where Ruger was, water splashed onto the floor. I looked down at the little puddle and wondered if some of Randy's sweat was in there too.

Which was when my eyes landed on something shiny just underneath the radiator.

Something gold. "My ring!" I yelped. Somebody must've kicked it under there.

The other kids turned to look at me as I ran to the radiator and retrieved my ring from under it.

I slid the ring back on my finger. Then I cleared my throat. "Hey, look," I said, "I'm sorry for freaking out. But this ring really means a lot to me."

This time, no one froze. No one spoke. No one was even looking at me anymore.

They'd all gone back to boxing.

FIVE

I fell for Cyrus's photography before I fell for him.

I still enjoy remembering how it happened. One afternoon last January, my mom asked me to return some books to the library. The drop-off box outside was frozen shut, so I had to go inside. Otherwise I'd never have seen the exhibit—prize-winning photographs by Montreal high school students. I was in a rush, but one photo—mounted between two sheets of glass and suspended from the ceiling—made me stop. Four brightly colored balloons trapped between two telephone wires, a perfectly blue summer sky in the background.

I paused to admire the photo's colors and composition—the intersection of ovals and horizontal lines. But what I liked even more was that whoever had taken this photo had noticed those balloons caught between the wires in the first place. I knew that person had to be special.

"Love." I didn't realize I'd said the word out loud.

Not until a lanky guy with a camera hanging around his neck touched my elbow. "Did you just say *love*?" he asked. His hair was short and curly.

"Uh, yeah." I knew I was blushing. "I really love this photo."

The guy grinned.

"Did you ta—?" I started to ask.

"I took it," he said at the same time.

Which made us both laugh.

He reached out to shake my hand. "I'm Cyrus Hollis. I can see you like bold colors." He was looking at my hair. "Very cool," he said.

"I'm Tessa McPhail."

"I've seen you around Tyndale," he said.

"You go to Tyndale? How come I never saw you?"

"I guess I'm easy to miss—unlike you. I mostly hang out on the second floor—with other kids in the camera club."

We went for hot chocolate that afternoon. I tried not to let on how much I liked him. But the library books gave me away. They were still in a pile by my feet when we got up to leave the café. Cyrus noticed them. "Hey, I think you forgot all about returning your library books."

"They're not mine. They're my mom's."

The next weekend, we went skating at Murray Hill Park. I waited until we were taking off our skates to tell Cyrus about my tagging and how I'd had some trouble with the police.

At first, he didn't say anything, which made me worry that he might not want to keep seeing me. But then he leaned in close and whispered, "I never thought I'd want to kiss a juvenile delinquent."

And then Cyrus had kissed me. It was only when he was walking me home that afternoon that he said, "Just so we're clear about this, tagging isn't art."

I admired—sometimes even envied—Cyrus's passion for photography. But I have to admit, there were times I wished he didn't lug his camera—a Canon DSLR—and his tripod every single place we went. Like Friday night at Girouard Park, after we'd had dinner with his parents.

Girouard Park is halfway between Cyrus's house in Westmount and the apartment in Notre-Dame-de-Grâce where Mom and I live. We were sitting on "our" bench when Cyrus took his hand off my shoulder and rested it on his camera case. "You shouldn't have told them that story about how the dog got its name," he said.

Though I didn't feel like admitting it to Cyrus, I knew I'd gone too far by telling his parents about Ruger. Mrs. Hollis had nearly choked on her green beans.

Usually, I liked how predictable the Hollises were— how they called each other *darling* and how I knew, even before I rang the doorbell, what we'd be having for dinner, since Mrs. Hollis made the same thing every Friday—roast chicken, potatoes and green beans, apple pie with ice cream for dessert.

But that night, everything about the Hollises had gotten on my nerves. It started when they asked how things were going for me at *that school*. Neither of them called it New Directions. I recognized the irony. I wanted to be able to complain about New Directions, but it bothered me if anyone else spoke about the school in a disrespectful way.

"It sure beat your mother telling the story of how she inherited the gravy bowl from her great aunt—or supervising while you ate all your beans."

I was relieved when Cyrus laughed. "You make a good point."

Except for some homeless guy arguing with himself under a lamppost, we had the park to ourselves. The cedar bushes made the air smell sweet and clean. I rested my head on Cyrus's shoulder and looked up at the stars. There weren't many in the sky that night, but the ones that were there were unusually bright.

When Cyrus leaned forward and took the camera off his neck, I knew he was about to kiss me. Even so, I felt him keeping one eye on his equipment. Did he really think the homeless guy was going to grab it?

My mood improved when I felt Cyrus's lips brush against mine. Kissing Cyrus was like having an amazing conversation.

He asked me questions with his kisses. I answered with mine.

Eventually, though, we had to go back to the other kind of conversation.

"Tessa," Cyrus whispered into my hair, "I don't know about that school you're going to..."

I pulled away from him. "You're right. You don't know anything about my school. And you know who you sound like? Your parents. The school I go to"—I guess I wasn't ready yet to call it *my school*—"has a name. New Directions. Sure, I'd rather be at Tyndale hanging out with you, but that's not the way it is. I'm doing my best to get used to it, and you know what else? I could use a little support."

"Okay, okay," Cyrus said, pulling me back toward him. "Calm down, will you? I'm just wondering—how many other kids at New Directions have brothers who got shot?"

"I don't know. I haven't asked."

"Well, what are the other kids like?"

I thought maybe if I answered Cyrus's question, he'd understand why I didn't want him calling New Directions *that school*. "Well, there's another tagger. The one I told you about—the guy who draws these cool butterfly people. Pretty Boy. His real name's Percy. There're two other girls besides me: Jasmine—she's Asian—and Di. She's the one with the pit bull. Then there's Whisky and Randy. The boxing teacher, Big Ron, has a thing for nicknames. Jabbin' Jasmine, Lady Di, Randy Randy..."

I could feel Cyrus's shoulders tense up. "Randy Randy? As in horndog Randy? As in this guy's a player?"

"It's just a nickname."

"I don't like it."

"You don't have to."

"How do I know I can trust this Randy Randy?"

"Cut it out, Cyrus."

After that, neither of us said anything for a bit. We just sat looking at the stars. It was better than arguing.

Cyrus removed his camera from the case. Then he took off the lens cap and inspected the lens. "Want to see the photos I shot at Mount Royal?" he asked.

"Sure." Cyrus knew I couldn't resist his photos.

He hit the Display button, and I leaned in to look.

"Love," I said, and we both laughed. It was a photo of a tall bare tree perched on the edge of a narrow rocky cliff. "Most people would've walked by that tree without noticing it. But not you."

"Thanks," Cyrus said. "Wait till you see the next one."

The next one looked a lot like the last one. "How does this one make you feel?" Cyrus asked.

"Lonely." It was a beautiful photograph, but it did make me feel lonely.

"That's it." Cyrus sounded pleased, as if I'd given the correct answer. "Me too. That was the feeling I was aiming for...What about this one?"

We must have spent an hour looking at Cyrus's photos, talking about how they made us feel. Sometimes I thought photography was Cyrus's way of telling me things he couldn't say in words.

"Tessa..." Cyrus began.

I bristled. I could tell from the way he'd started his sentence by saying my name that he was about to make another annoying remark.

"I know you're trying to get used to New Directions, and I want to be supportive"—Cyrus paused, and I could feel the *but* coming—"but I still don't get a good feeling about that place. I think the boxing is making you more...well... aggressive. And Randy Randy..."

If this was Cyrus's idea of being supportive, he wasn't doing a very good job of it. It wasn't like I had any other options. And what gave him the right to judge me like that? I nudged his elbow. I didn't mean to knock his camera out of his hands, but I did. I was relieved when it landed on the bench and didn't go crashing to the ground.

Cyrus grabbed the camera and inspected it for scratches or dents. Then he looked up at me. "See what I mean?"

I got up from the bench. I looked down at my feet and realized that I'd gone into fighting stance. Left foot at one o'clock, right foot at two. "I'm glad your camera's okay," I told Cyrus, "but I've gotta go. Big Ron's offered me an extra boxing session tomorrow. I need to be up early."

SIX

From the stairway, I could hear Big Ron's booming voice. "It's easy to be a boozer," he was saying, which is how I knew he was talking to Whisky, "but it's hard to stay disciplined and lead the clean life. What you need to look for are natural things that make you feel good. Not phony, masking things like alcohol."

Whisky must've been glad when I walked into the gym. If not for me, Big Ron's lecture would have gone on even longer. Whisky nodded in my direction without missing a beat on the punching bag. When he socked the bag hard, I twitched. Luckily, the twitching didn't last very long.

I thought since it was Saturday, Big Ron might go easy on the warm-ups. But he didn't. This time, I knew better than to argue when he lost count of the number of jumping jacks I'd done.

I needed to stop to catch my breath after those jumping jacks. "Do you come in every Saturday?" I asked Big Ron. Even after knowing him for only a week, I'd already figured out that the one way to get a break was to get him talking.

"Not every Saturday. I may be obese, but that doesn't mean I don't have a life. I got friends, I go out on a date now and then. But when I can, I like to keep the gym open Saturdays. Do a little extra work with a newcomer like you. Keep the troublemakers off the streets—and away from all manner of poisons." He jerked his head toward Whisky.

"So I guess you really enjoy training teenagers…"

I was trying to come up with another question when Big Ron gave me a stern look. "You wouldn't be trying to distract me, would you, Tessa Something-or-Other?"

"Uh, of course not."

"All the same, gimme another twenty jumping jacks."

After leg stretches, we worked on my fighting stance. "Soon that position'll become automatic," Big Ron said. I could have told him about how I'd gone into fighting stance when I'd argued with Cyrus, but I didn't feel like sharing personal stuff with Big Ron.

Big Ron also wanted to see my straight punches. "Still a little stiff," he said. "You need to loosen up. That's important when you're throwing your punches but also when you're getting punched. If you're stiff, the impact is a helluva lot worse. When you're relaxed, you absorb a blow—like a sponge.

I bet you never thought you'd be learning how to take punches, did you, Tessa Something-or-Other?"

I had to admit, Big Ron was right.

Whisky was still whacking the bag, throwing body shots. "These are my favorite," he said when he caught me looking at him. "They do a lot of harm, and they don't leave marks."

Whisky was sober. Otherwise, his punches would've been sloppy. But I still smelled alcohol. That's when I realized it had to be coming from his sweat. Imagine drinking so much that even your sweat smells like booze!

Whisky wiped his forehead with a hand towel he took out of his backpack. "I'm going to the *dépanneur*," he said, reaching for his baseball cap. "I need something to drink."

"You better be getting Gatorade—not beer," Big Ron called out as Whisky shut the gym doors behind him.

I was practicing straight punches in front of the mirror. "Back foot in!" Big Ron bellowed. "Rotate those hips!"

He leaned forward, resting his chin in his hands. "There's something I been meaning to ask you, Tessa Something-or-Other." Big Ron looked right at me, and his voice was softer than usual. "I notice you get kinda jumpy here. I saw you twitch before when Whisky was hitting the bag. You freaked out when I grazed your jaw the other day. I'm going to be straight with you, 'cause that's the way I am. I'm thinking you been smacked around. You want to talk to me about it?"

"Nope," I said as I threw another straight punch.

"Are you telling me you were never smacked around?"

I let my hands drop to my sides. "That's exactly what I'm telling you." I really hoped that would put an end to the discussion.

Only it was obviously against Big Ron's philosophy to give up without a fight. And not just in the boxing ring. "So why the hell are you so jumpy?" he asked.

I took a deep breath. "I was trampled during the 2008 hockey riot."

Big Ron gestured to the lawn chair next to his. "Why don't you have a seat," he said, "and tell me what happened."

I didn't feel like giving him the details. It was too personal. On the other hand, I didn't see how I was going to get out of it. I decided I'd tell Big Ron something but keep it short.

"I was with my mom. We got separated in the mob. Two guys got into a fight. One landed on me." There—that was all he needed to know.

"Landed on you?" I had the feeling he was trying to picture it.

"Yup. I was pretty bruised up afterward, but nothing was broken."

"Uh-huh," Big Ron said. I could tell he knew there was more to the story.

"My mom got hurt too. She was trying to reach me when some guy banged into her. He broke her glasses and her cheek got cut up. There was a lot of blood…"

"A lot of blood? And you were only…what, eleven? That must've scared the daylights outta you."

"It did."

"I'm guessing you felt responsible."

"I did."

"So you think that's why boxing makes you jittery?" I felt Big Ron watching my face, waiting to see my reaction.

"I guess."

He looked me in the eye again. "I don't."

"What do you mean, you don't?" I hoped Big Ron would know from the way I said it that I didn't like him prying into my personal history.

"I mean I don't. I've worked with a lot of teenagers in my time. The ones that are jumpy like you, they've been beaten up—or else they've seen someone else get beaten up. And I mean really beaten up."

When I crossed my arms over my chest, I could feel my shoulders tensing up again. "I don't know what you're talking about. Would you mind if we got back to my workout?"

Big Ron shrugged. "Whatever you say, Tessa Something-or-Other. Whatever you say." He got up from his chair and waddled over to his supply closet. He rummaged inside for a minute, then turned and threw me a pair of black boxing gloves. The gloves were so worn, they were duct-taped together in a few places. "Put those on," Big Ron said. "I think you're ready for the punching bag."

Whacking the bag was more work than punching air, but it also felt better than I'd expected. "How come when I punch the bag," I asked Big Ron, "it doesn't make the *bam-bam* sound it makes when Whisky does it?"

"Give it time," Big Ron said. "Lots of things take time, Tessa Something-or-Other." Was it my imagination or did he look at me a little too long when he said that?

Big Ron counted out each punch. "Not so fast," he said when I hit the bag too soon.

At first, I counted in my head too, but then I stopped counting and tried to concentrate on just the punches. It took a while, but I started to get the rhythm. So what if my punches still didn't make the sound Whisky's did?

One memory had come back to me during Miss Lebrun's writing exercises. I never expected that another one would come back when I was hitting the punching bag. But that's exactly how it happened.

If I'd picked the number thirteen out of Whisky's cap, I might have remembered this scene instead. It was the summer after middle school, before I started at Tyndale. This girl named Rachel was staying with her grandparents, down the street from us. I knew there was something strange about Rachel, though I didn't know what. She had dark eyes that went all bulgy when she talked about her favorite subject: the weather.

Rachel didn't just talk about the temperature and whether or not it might rain. She talked about stuff like barometric pressure and the humidex, which is an index used in Canada to describe how hot the weather feels to the average person. I know because Rachel explained it to me. Lots of times.

Rachel's grandparents sent her to the local day camp— probably because they couldn't bear listening to her babble all day. Rachel and I were in the same group at camp. It was Mom's idea that Rachel and I walk home together since we lived so close to each other. I tried getting out of it, but Mom insisted. "Rachel needs a kind friend," she said. "You be that friend, Tessa."

So I got stuck walking home from camp every afternoon with Rachel. Which is how I learned about barometric pressure and the humidex.

"What's up, Weathergirl?" That's what the other girls in our group called her—Weathergirl.

Rachel wouldn't even realize they were teasing.

"Nothing much," she'd say, flashing them her goofy smile. "What about you?"

That would only make them meaner. They'd follow us down the block. "You know what you are, Weathergirl?" they'd call out. "You're a freak!"

"You're no better," they'd say to me. "You're friends with a freak."

I wanted to tell them I wasn't really friends with Rachel. But I could never say it—not in front of Rachel.

I'd tug on Rachel's arm to make her walk faster, but she'd say, "Don't!" and shake my hand away. Rachel didn't like it when people got too close—not even her grandparents.

"Well then, hurry up!" I'd hiss, but she'd turn around, checking to see if the girls were still there—which just gave them time to come closer.

One afternoon, two of the girls sprinted ahead of us. I didn't understand what they were up to until they stopped and turned around, their eyes shining. That was when I realized Rachel and I were trapped. Four girls had formed a circle around us.

"What's wrong with you exactly, Weathergirl?" Angela, the leader, asked.

"There's n-nothing wrong with me." Rachel didn't sound so sure about it.

Angela stepped closer to us. Then she looked at her friends, telling them something with her eyes. They tightened the circle around us.

"She doesn't like it when people get too close," I said, but that only made them laugh.

Rachel's dark eyes bulged, this time from fear.

"Leave us alone!" she called out.

One girl took her phone out from the back pocket of her shorts. I didn't think much of it at the time.

Angela wasn't the first one to lay a finger on Rachel. It was Megan, Angela's second in command. Megan flicked Rachel's elbow. It couldn't have hurt, but Rachel cried out just the same.

The circle closed in tighter.

"Crybaby!"

"Loser Weathergirl!"

"What's wrong with you, Weathergirl?"

They weren't after me; they were after Rachel. When I turned my head, I could see a narrow opening in the circle, right behind me. If I was quick, I might be able to get away.

Angela and Megan and another girl were blocking Rachel's way. Even if Rachel was fast—which she wasn't— she wouldn't have been able to escape.

Angela was the one who spotted the giant wheeled recycling bin at the end of someone's driveway. "Get that bin!" she shouted to one of the others.

I didn't know what they wanted with the bin. I didn't care. All I cared about was getting away from Angela and her friends—and from Rachel. I remember thinking that everything that was happening was Rachel's fault.

No one seemed to notice—or care—when I made a run for it. I could hear Rachel blubbering. "Don't!" she kept saying over and over again.

I ducked behind a parked car. My heart was pounding, and I needed to catch my breath. Besides, if I'd kept running, I might have drawn attention to myself.

The other girls were laughing, jeering. "Is that a cumulus cloud?" one of the girls shrieked. "Well, is it?"

The bin was so big, it took two girls to turn it over to keep it from moving.

By that point, Rachel had curled up on the ground in the fetal position, so it took only one girl—Megan—to shove Rachel into the recycling bin.

Angela supervised, hands on her hips. "Let's take Weathergirl for a ride!" she squealed. Three of the girls hurled themselves against the bin and started pushing it down the street, faster and faster. The sounds of the plastic wheels jiggling over the pavement and the girls' screams drowned out Rachel's sobs.

That was when I took off. I didn't see the rest until later—on YouTube. By then, Rachel's grandparents had sent her home.

"Why aren't you punching?" Big Ron was asking me.

I didn't know how long I'd been standing there, my hand over my mouth.

"I think I need a break," I told Big Ron.

Only it wasn't the boxing I needed to recover from. It was the memory of my own weakness.

SEVEN

"So how you liking New Directions?"

I nearly fell off my seat on the metro. I was on my way to school and I'd been sitting next to a scrawny guy in a black baseball cap for at least two stops. How could I not have recognized Pretty Boy?

"Where's your boa?" I asked him.

"I keep it in my backpack when I take public transport. Sometimes it's better to keep a low profile. So how are you liking New Directions?"

"It's a hellhole, but I guess I'm getting used to it. How 'bout you? You seem to like it—except for your sleep disorder."

"It's better for me than my old school. The kids there didn't think much of my feather boa, if you know what I mean. And Big Ron's been good for me."

"I know. I saw you punch out that guy—the one who was sitting on top of you. You were pretty impressive."

"Oh, him…garden-variety homophobe. I tried to drag you away before the cops showed up."

"I remember—kind of. Thanks for trying."

The metro stopped at the Côte-Sainte-Catherine station and more passengers got on. Pretty Boy gave his seat to an elderly woman with a cane. The woman didn't bother to thank him. She just plunked herself down on the seat. I hoped no one would trip over her cane.

Pretty Boy grabbed the metal bar so he could steady himself when the metro lurched forward.

"I've seen your tags," he said. "TM, right? In the trade-mark oval? I like the concept. Is that what landed you at New Directions—tagging?"

"Yup. You too?"

Pretty Boy looked away. "Yeah," he said to the silver metro doors, "that and some other stuff."

We sat in silence as the stops went by.

We got off at the Pie-IX station. "Gimme a second," Pretty Boy said when we were approaching the escalator. He reached into his backpack for his feather boa.

I hadn't seen this one before. It was bright orange. "Nice," I told him.

He draped it twice around his neck, then let it hang down his back.

When we reached the block where New Directions was,

we could see the woman from next door outside, sweeping her walkway. She shook her head when she noticed Pretty Boy's feather boa.

Pretty Boy grabbed one end of the feather boa and waved it at the woman. "Good morning to you too!" he called out.

It was only seven forty. Jasmine and Whisky were waiting on the porch. Whisky reeked of alcohol and cigarettes. I had a feeling Big Ron wouldn't be too pleased.

"You gonna let us in or what?" Whisky said to Pretty Boy.

Pretty Boy checked the time on his cell phone. "Big Ron and Miss Lebrun'll be here by five to eight. That's only fifteen minutes. Besides, you smell like you could use some airing out."

"Come on," Whisky said, using one hand as a visor. "The sun is killing my eyes."

Pretty Boy sighed as he reached into his pocket and pulled out a piece of wire, coiled up tight. He uncoiled the wire, straightening it with his fingers. "The things I do for my peeps," he muttered as he headed for the narrow walkway between New Directions and the house next door.

Whisky flipped open his phone. "I'm timing you, Pretty Boy!" he called after him, laughing. "Your record is four minutes, twenty seconds."

Pretty Boy beat his record. Exactly four minutes and twelve seconds later, the front door to the school flew open and there was Pretty Boy, his orange boa draped over his shoulders. He extended one arm toward us like a ring-master introducing a circus act.

Neither Big Ron or Miss Lebrun said anything about it when they turned up—Miss Lebrun on her bike, Big Ron in a pickup truck—and we were already inside. Pretty Boy had turned on the coffee machine in the kitchen, and Miss Lebrun poured herself a cup.

Big Ron opened the fridge and took out a carton of orange juice. The fridge smelled sour. "Maybe you should go home and sleep it off," Big Ron told Whisky.

"This miserable place is my home," Whisky said.

Jasmine pretended to play the violin, slicing the air with an imaginary bow.

I sat down at the table next to Jasmine. "How come you're not wearing your precious ring?" she asked me. "I hope no underage delinquent stole it."

"I decided to take a break—from the ring. I'm sorry for freaking out the way I did. I was an idiot."

Jasmine flicked at a bit of dirt on the kitchen table. Her black nail polish was starting to chip off. "No biggie," she said. "We're all idiots sometimes. Welcome to the club."

Whisky leaned back so far in his chair that the front legs lifted off the ground. "I'll bet you anything Miss Lebrun was never an idiot. Anytime. Right, Miss Lebrun?"

Miss Lebrun smiled. "That's right, William."

Though I'd never have admitted it to anyone else, I was actually starting to look forward to Miss Lebrun's writing exercises. I liked starting my day on paper. Miss Lebrun had told us she got some of her ideas on her bike rides to school.

That morning, she told us to write the numbers one through twenty-five down the side of a page. "We're doing a list. Are you ready?" Sometimes I thought Miss Lebrun needed to ease up on the coffee. "Lists are a useful remedy for writer's block," she continued.

As usual, Pretty Boy was slumped over his desk. Now he looked up from his morning nap. "Who said we had writer's block?" he asked.

"You want us to make a list of everything we want for Christmas?" Di called out. She was sitting to the other side of me. "I could do that list easy. I want a new jean jacket and an iPod. And one of those charm bracelets the Westmount girls wear."

"I had a different sort of list in mind," Miss Lebrun said, "though your idea has possibilities, Diane. Today, I want you each to write a list of how you spend your time. All the things you do in a day—or a week. How we spend our time says a lot about us—about our values. Just make your lists as quickly as you can, without thinking too much."

"I like that part," Pretty Boy said, and the rest of us laughed.

"You can even repeat items on your list," Miss Lebrun added. "The main thing is not to censor yourselves."

Whisky made a snorting sound. "You mean Randy can write *getting laid* twenty-five times?" he asked.

"It's better than writing *getting loaded* twenty-five times," Randy called from the back of the room.

"All right, gentlemen," Miss Lebrun said. "Let's settle down and get to work."

I wrote *Making out with Cyrus*, but then I crossed it out.

I was still ticked off with him. After I'd left the park that night, he'd followed me for a while, walking a few steps behind me, but I'd ignored him, and eventually he gave up and turned around. Though it didn't make sense, I was mad at him for that too—for abandoning me.

So I wrote *Tagging* instead. Only writing that seemed weird too. I hadn't tagged in ages. Not since the police had picked me up that night in June. Mom had made me promise to stop. So far, I'd kept my word.

Looking at art books.

Looking at books about street art.

Watching people.

Taking the metro.

Doing chores around the apartment. Dishes. Laundry.

The list was getting easier. I liked the feeling of my pen moving almost like a paintbrush across the page.

I heard Di drop her pen on her desk. I was surprised she had finished the exercise so quickly. I thought she did everything in slow motion.

When I turned to look at her, she was getting up from her desk. Her shoulders were hunched, and she had one hand over her mouth. My first thought was that something she'd written on her list had upset her.

Miss Lebrun, who had been writing her own list, looked up too. "Diane, is there someth—?"

Di rested one hand on my desk. Then she rushed to the front of the classroom where Miss Lebrun's desk was.

Di's hand was still over her mouth, but now she made this gross gulping sound. The color had drained from her face, and her hand was so pale it looked like you could see through it.

That's when I knew Di was headed to the black metal garbage can next to Miss Lebrun's desk. The one where we dumped our apple cores and wadded-up chewing gum.

Di's arm shot out as she reached for the garbage can and lifted it from the ground.

Then she vomited—a jet of yellow and white that looked like chewed-up corn and smelled worse—right into the can.

"Basket!" Whisky called out.

By then, Di was on her knees, doubled over the garbage can. She'd finished vomiting, but her shoulders were still heaving.

Miss Lebrun leaned over Di and patted her shoulder. "It's okay," Miss Lebrun told her. "Everything's going to be okay."

Pretty Boy scooped up the garbage can without saying a word and left the room. I could tell from the way he was scrunching his face that he was trying not to inhale.

Di wiped away the vomit around her mouth. When she could stand again, she followed Pretty Boy out of the room. She must have wanted to rinse out her mouth—and her peasant blouse.

Before the door closed, we heard Pretty Boy say, "So, Lady Di, what's it gonna be? A boy—or a girl?"

EIGHT

"There's something I've always wanted to know," Whisky called from the back of the classroom when I got up from my seat. "How come girls go to the bathroom in packs?"

Jasmine had rushed out after Di without asking for Miss Lebrun's permission. I guess this qualified as an emergency.

"I'm not in a pack. I need to pee," I told Whisky. Then I turned to Miss Lebrun. "Desperately. If you don't let me go, I'll have to pee on the floor."

Pretty Boy turned to look at me from between his elbows, where he was resting his head after coming back to class. "Not a good idea," he said. "Besides, we've had suffi- cient exposure to bodily fluids for one day."

Di and Jasmine must have been talking, but they stopped when I walked into the bathroom. Di was standing in front of the mirror in her bra, reapplying her eyeliner.

Jasmine was scrubbing Di's blouse in the sink, soaping it up, then scrubbing some more.

I couldn't help peeking at Lady Di's belly. It looked as flat as mine. I wondered how far along she was.

"Sorry," I told them. "I really need to pee."

"Well go ahead and pee then," Jasmine muttered, without looking up from the sink.

"I think I got it all out," I heard her tell Di when I was inside the stall. "It just needs to dry out a little."

"I need a cigarette. Bad," Di said.

"You shouldn't smoke," I said from the stall. "It's bad for the baby."

"You should mind your own business, Tessa Something-or-Other. Besides, Di's not even sure she's going to keep it," Jasmine said.

"Wanna hang out with us for a bit?" Di asked when I was washing my hands. The bathroom still smelled like vomit.

Jasmine rolled her eyes. "I can't believe you asked her that," she said, as if I wasn't right there.

"You mean hang out *here*?" I asked.

"Why not?" Di and Jasmine had planted themselves on the steel counter by the sink. Jasmine had hung Di's blouse over one of the stall doors. Now Di lit up a cigarette and began puffing away. I figured it was best not to offer any more warnings—or to remind her of the no-smoking rule at New Directions.

Di passed the cigarette to Jasmine, who took a puff, then offered it to me.

"Thanks," I said. "I don't smoke."

"Why am I not surprised?" Di said. "I suppose you don't have unprotected sex either." She slid over on the counter to make room for me.

"You're right," I said, squeezing into the spot. "I don't. How come you did?"

"My boyfriend. He hates condoms. He said he'd make sure I wouldn't get pregnant. But I'm getting used to the idea—sort of." Di looked down at her belly. Then she patted it.

"He's not your boyfriend," Jasmine said.

"He is too my boyfriend."

"Is it Randy?" I asked.

That cracked them up. I started to laugh too, not because it was so funny, but because I needed to laugh.

"Lady Di is dumb," Jasmine said, "but not *that* dumb. Randy's got too many girlfriends to count."

"My boyfriend doesn't go here. Sal's older." Di sounded proud.

Jasmine plucked the cigarette from between Di's lips. "Old enough to know better. So"—she turned to look at me—"you got a thing for Randy?"

"Uh...no," I said. "Of course not. I've got a boyfriend. Sort of. He does photography. One of his photos was even in an exhibit."

"If he's so great, how come he's only *sort of* your boyfriend?" Di seemed glad to change the subject.

"I don't know. It's hard to explain. He gets kind of jealous."

"Do you give him reason to get jealous?" Jasmine asked.

It was a good question. "No," I told her. "I don't."

"Well then that sucks," Jasmine said.

"It's not just that. We're different. Sometimes he makes me feel like I'm wasting my life. Like I don't have focus."

"*Focus*? Maybe that's because he's a photographer." Jasmine guffawed at her own joke.

I didn't know why I was telling them all this. Maybe it had something to do with being together in such a small space, with the air gray from cigarette smoke. It felt like we were in another world.

"*You* wasting your life? I'd hate to know what he'd say about *my* life," Di said.

Jasmine rolled her eyes. She did that a lot. "Who cares what he'd say? You don't even know the guy."

Instead of answering Jasmine, Di turned back to me. "Where d'you know Pretty Boy from, anyhow?"

"From tagging."

"You're a tagger?" Di seemed impressed.

"I used to be. I promised my mom I'd stop."

"She promised her mom she'd stop," Jasmine said in a nasal imitation of me.

Di nudged my elbow. "Don't mind her," she said. "She wishes she still had a mom."

Jasmine's eyes narrowed. "I have an aunt. That's like having a mom."

"Not with your aunt, it isn't," Di said.

Jasmine took a long drag on the cigarette. "Did you know Pretty Boy's been in juvie?" she asked me.

"For tagging?"

"No, not for tagging. For breaking and entering. B and E's are his specialty," Jasmine said.

His specialty. No wonder Pretty Boy had been able to get into the school this morning.

"He was the runt in the family. He's got three older brothers—all big guys. Because he was so puny, they used to look for houses where the windows were a bit open, then make him slip inside. Next thing you knew, *voilà!* He'd be opening the front door and letting them in. You know what I heard? That they never even gave him a cut of what they stole—just paid him in weed."

"Where are Pretty Boy's brothers now?" I asked.

"Two are out. One's still in university," Di said.

"In university?" So the story had a happy ending. "What's he studying?" I asked.

Jasmine shook her head. "Not that kind of university, dumbass." She wasn't talking about McGill or Concordia or the University of Toronto. She meant prison.

Someone was rapping on the bathroom door.

"Big Ron," Jasmine said, stubbing out the cigarette in the sink, then running the water so the butt disappeared down the drain.

"I hate to interrupt your morning meeting, ladies"—Big Ron's voice boomed through the door—"but you're wanted upstairs. And open the window in there, will ya? I don't know what's worse—the puke or the cigarettes."

I had to stand on the counter to open the window.

There was nowhere to look but up, so I found myself staring into the angry face of the woman next door. She had just stepped out on her upstairs balcony. Her frizzy hair was tied back in a bun. A plastic clothes hamper was propped between her arms, and she had a clothespin between her lips. She noticed me at the same moment I noticed her. She took the clothespin from her mouth. "You're smoking in there, aren't you?" she shouted. "I can smell it from here. Your school's a no-smoking facility, you know!"

"Tell that bitch to mind her own business!" Jasmine said loudly.

"Stop it, Jasmine! You'll only make things worse!" Di said.

I was tempted to shut the window, but I didn't. Instead, I looked out at the dried-up backyard and the rusted-out basketball hoop. Something seemed to be missing, though at first I wasn't sure what.

Then it occurred to me. The sunflowers. Where was the row of giant sunflowers that had been lined up by the fence?

"What happened to your sunflowers?" I called out.

If the woman's face had been made of stone, I swear it would have cracked. "What do you think happened to them?" she shouted. "One of you delinquents destroyed them!" She turned and went back into her house, slamming the door behind her.

Pretty Boy wasn't the only one on the block with anger-management issues. Still, I couldn't help feeling a little sorry for the woman. I missed the sunflowers too. Looking at them had made me forget what a crappy neighborhood we were in. Maybe they'd had the same effect on her and that was why she missed them so much.

When we left the bathroom, Big Ron was back in the gym, hitting one of the punching bags. I didn't know he still trained. He'd left the door to the gym open. He kept punching as we walked by. "Hey, Lady Di," he called out, without breaking the rhythm of his punches. "If you decide to keep the baby—and, of course, that's your call—but if you do, you won't be going in the ring for a while. We don't want to risk you getting injured or injuring the baby. But you can keep doing the warm-ups with the rest of the group till your seventh month. Jabbin' Jasmine, you'll need someone new to spar with. Which means that you, Tessa Something-or-Other, just got yourself enrolled in my accelerated program."

NINE

Big Ron wasn't kidding about his accelerated boxing program. Every afternoon, when our class had boxing, he spent half an hour training me on my own. After straight punches, I learned uppercuts. Then Big Ron added in legwork. "Small steps," he'd bellow from his lawn chair as I practiced my punches while moving forward and backward. He threw his arms up into the air. "What'd I tell you about keeping your back foot in position?"

By the time we were into the second week of the accelerated program, I was starting to feel frustrated. I was hoping to have improved more by then. School subjects had always come easily to me, and I didn't like the feeling of being a slow learner. I noticed that sometimes I messed up even more after Big Ron had corrected me. Now, when I stopped to readjust my back foot, I forgot to keep punching. Then it was hard to get my rhythm back. What if I never got the hang of it?

"You're thinking too much, Tessa Something-or-Other. That's your problem!" Big Ron said, shaking his head.

"I can't help it!" I told him.

That only made Big Ron more frustrated with me. "Of course you can help it! Now try again—without thinking so much!"

Every training session ended at the punching bag. By then I was drained, and the muscles in my arms and legs were achier than when I had the flu. All I wanted to do was plant myself on a bench at the side of the gym. Sometimes I imagined collapsing on the floor and lying spread-eagled beside the punching bag. Man, that would feel good!

But Big Ron would never have let me. "All right, Tessa Something-or-Other," he'd say when I got to the punching bag, "show me what you've got left."

Once I tried telling him I had nothing left, but that just made him laugh. "Don't you think boxers feel like that in the ring too—like they've got nothing left? That's when it really counts, Tessa Something-or-Other—when you've got nothing left and you still keep fighting. That's what boxing's all about."

So I'd punch that bag even when I swore I couldn't. Sometimes I'd get a second wind. It helped to think about stuff that made me mad—the way Cyrus's parents wouldn't call New Directions by its name, homophobes like the one who'd tried to beat up Pretty Boy. Sometimes I even thought about the night of the hockey riot and about Rachel. There was nothing I could have done to help Mom the night of the hockey riot, but I knew I should have tried to help Rachel. And I hadn't. I'd been too scared…and too busy looking out for myself.

I'd smash the front of the beat-up boxing gloves into the punching bag and let it all out. "That's my girl!" Big Ron would say, high-fiving me when I was done.

"I'll be honest with you," he said to me one day. "You're not a natural, but you've got something I can't teach."

"What's that?" I knew I wasn't a natural, but it still smarted to hear Big Ron say so.

He nodded his head and looked at me with something like respect. "You're a fighter, Tessa Something-or-Other. I'll give you that."

I don't think I'd ever had a better compliment.

I wasn't ready to spar, but watching the others take each other on in the ring was part of learning to box. Sometimes I still winced when I heard the sounds of punching or watched the sparring, but not as much as before.

Sometimes I caught myself analyzing the sparring sessions. I noticed how Pretty Boy was good at keeping up his guard, how deft Randy's footwork was. Noticing these things gave me a little distance from my old feelings—the fear and panic I'd always had when I was confronted by any kind of violence. I hoped that meant I was getting stronger in ways that had nothing to do with muscle mass.

Randy and Whisky were dancing around each other in the ring. They were both wearing headgear—soft, padded leather helmets that made them look like gladiators. When Whisky opened his mouth, I could see his red plastic mouthguard.

Big Ron was standing outside the ring, supervising from the ropes. His eyes darted back and forth between his fighters. The rest of us watched from the other side. Two girls—both in miniskirts and wedge sneakers—were visiting from some other school. "Randy's groupies. There's plenty more where those two came from," Jasmine had said.

I was standing next to Jasmine and Di. Jasmine's eyes moved almost as quickly as Big Ron's; Di's hands were crossed over her belly. I wondered if that meant she was planning to keep the baby.

"Nice move!" Big Ron said when Whisky ducked, narrowly escaping Randy's right hook.

"Looking good!" Big Ron added when Randy came back with another punch.

Randy's groupies squealed. If he noticed, he didn't show it.

Watching the sparring made me realize that there were all kinds of boxers. Whisky moved his head a lot when he boxed.

Randy was nimble on his feet—*That boy dances on his toes*, Big Ron liked to say about him.

Whisky didn't have Randy's speed. I wondered if Whisky's bad habits had something to do with that. When I'd passed him on the front porch of the school that morning, the alcohol fumes were so strong I'd had to hold my breath.

"How come Whisky drinks so much?" I whispered to Jasmine.

She answered without lifting her eyes from the action inside the ring. "It's in his genes. The dad drinks. The grandma drinks. I once heard Whisky say drinking killed his mom. Cirrhosis of the liver." She said it as factually as if she were doing an oral presentation in our classroom upstairs.

I shook my head. "That's horrible."

"Can you quit yakking and let me watch this?"

Whisky and Randy both must have been protecting themselves, because they'd gotten into a clinch. They were holding on to each other so tightly, neither of them could break loose.

Big Ron moved in closer to the ropes. "Break and step back!" he shouted to the two fighters.

Randy muttered something to Whisky. I wasn't sure, but I thought I heard the words *useless* and *drunk*.

That's when Whisky gave Randy a shot in the face and said, "Deal with that, you fuckin' retard."

"Oh my god," one of the groupies said.

"Are you okay, Randy?" the other one asked.

I felt Jasmine tense up next to me. "Uh-oh," she whispered. "Randy doesn't like being reminded he's LD."

"LD?" I asked. I'd never heard the term before.

Di nudged my arm. "Learning disabled. Couldn't you tell?"

Now that I thought about it, I realized that Randy took longer than anyone else to copy Miss Lebrun's notes from the blackboard. And he was the only one in our class Miss Lebrun never called on to read out loud.

Big Ron's face was so red, it looked like an overripe tomato. "Hey, hey!" he said.

Randy's eyes flashed as he whacked Whisky back.

"Stop it! Now!" Big Ron bellowed. Only they didn't.

Pretty Boy, who also should have known better, was leaning over the ropes, egging them on. "Get him, Randy!" he shouted, and then, "Way to go, Whisky!"

Part of me didn't want to look. Another part couldn't look away.

Big Ron panted as he hoisted himself over the ropes and into the ring. It was like watching a bear come out of hibernation. He got in between Whisky and Randy and, with his elbows, pushed them both back into the ropes. He might be overweight, but Big Ron was strong.

All three of them were panting now.

Sweat from Big Ron's forehead dribbled down to the rubber floor mat. "You're here to help each other," he shouted. "Not destroy each other! You got that?"

Then he looked over at Whisky. "I'm the coach in this gym, and when I say something, you listen. I told you to step back."

Whisky's eyes were bloodshot. "He called me a drunk."

"So what if he called you a drunk? You *are* a drunk! And you still gotta listen to what I say. You got that, Whisky?"

Whisky looked down at the floor. "Got it."

Then Big Ron turned to Randy. "You know you shouldn't have hit him back. You gotta let me take care of things around here. Understood?"

"Understood," Randy said, spitting out the word.

Big Ron shook his head. "I'm not even going to talk about the name-calling. You know why?" He glared at both of them. "Because this place is a high school. Not some friggin' day care."

Pretty Boy was the one who noticed the signs on our way home that afternoon. One was on a telephone pole; others were stapled to tree trunks. "Can you believe this shit?" Pretty Boy said as he tore the first sign off and tossed it into a garbage can. We walked a little farther and there was another one and then another. Those things were popping up like weeds.

There was a grainy photo of our school on the sign. Underneath, in giant black letters, were two questions:

Did you know that students at the New Directions Academy spend half the day boxing?

Are you going to let violent juvenile delinquents take over our neighborhood?

In smaller letters, there was a notice about an upcoming meeting—8:00 PM the following Thursday at the local community center.

"D'you think she put up the signs?" I asked Pretty Boy.

He knew who I meant—the woman who lived next door to the school.

"I'd bet my gay ass she did."

"Did you tear down her sunflowers?" I asked him. I was almost sure he had.

Pretty Boy grinned. "Now why would a nature lover like me do something like that?"

"We can't just keep tearing down the signs," I told him.

"I don't see why not." He tore down another one.

"She'll just put more up."

Pretty Boy made a growling sound. "What if she gets all her loser friends to sign her petition and they shut our school? Then what?"

I don't think Pretty Boy knew he was shouting, and if he did, he didn't care.

"I guess they'd have to move New Directions some-place else."

"You just don't get, it, do you, Tessa? If this shithole neighborhood doesn't want us, you think some other neighborhood will? The school board shuts down this place, we got nowhere to go. Do you hear me? Nowhere! Not all of us have cushy lives like you do, Tessa, with a mommy who packs her lunch in an insulated bag."

I did have an insulated lunch bag. And sometimes, when I was in a hurry, my mom packed my lunch for me. Now I wondered if there were other things about me Pretty Boy had been noticing—and holding against me.

He was still ranting. "For some of us, having nowhere to go doesn't just mean we won't get out of high school. It means trouble. Big trouble." Now he sounded more worried than angry. Was he worried that if he wasn't in school, his older brothers would pressure him to do more B & E's?

"In that case," I said, "we need a plan to save New Directions."

From the way Pretty Boy looked at me, I could tell he was surprised.

"I thought you hated New Directions…you said it was a hellhole."

"It is a hellhole," I said, bumping my elbow into his. "But hey, it's our hellhole. And like you said, where would you guys be without it?"

Pretty Boy walked over to a pole with another poster on it. He was about to tear it down, but he stopped himself. "You don't happen to have a better plan in mind, do you?"

It just so happened that a better plan was beginning to hatch in my head. Thinking too much might be a problem in boxing, but in other situations, it can come in handy. "How about we organize our own public meeting? At New Directions. So the neighbors can see what we're really like."

Pretty Boy whooped. "What we're *really* like? That, Tessa Something-or-Other, might not be such a good idea!"

TEN

Mr. Turner loved the idea. He'd come to New Directions for a meeting with Miss Lebrun and Big Ron, but when Miss Lebrun mentioned my plan, he wanted to meet right away with all of us.

"We'll make it an open house," he said, rubbing his head. "What the people in this neighborhood need is information. We'll do it next Tuesday night. That way it'll be a preemptive strike. Can I count on all of you to be present—and also to help prepare for the event?" he asked us. He was so excited that when the back of his shirt came untucked from his slacks, he didn't bother tucking it back in. "What we need is to get the neighbors on side. I'd like to hear any of your suggestions."

Randy raised his hand.

"Yes, Randall?" Mr. Turner said, nodding at Randy.

"I'm thinking…" Randy began. Ever since Jasmine had mentioned that Randy was LD, I'd started noticing how he spoke more slowly than any of us, as if he had to translate the words in his brain before he said them. "If this is about public relations"—Randy paused—"well, it might be a better move"—he paused again—"to make some of the students stay home."

Randy turned to look at Whisky, who glared back at him. They might have shaken hands after their sparring match, but we all knew they hadn't really settled things.

Di was looking down at her belly. It still looked perfectly flat to me. But maybe she was wondering whether she should stay home too.

Miss Lebrun cleared her throat. "I think it's important that each and every one of you is here on Tuesday night. You're all part of New Directions." She gave Randy a steely look when she said that.

After Mr. Turner left, Miss Lebrun organized us into teams of two. Pretty Boy and I were in charge of décor. "What I'd really like," Miss Lebrun told us, "is for the two of you to do some paintings. We could hang them on the walls. Right now, all we've got are posters about the dangers of drug abuse."

"And the importance of safe sex," I added.

"That too," Miss Lebrun said. "By the way, I have a little surprise for you two." She gestured for us to follow her to the supply closet at the back of our classroom. "There was a little extra money in the budget, so Mr. Turner gave me the okay to buy some art supplies." She reached deep into the closet, lugging out four giant canvases and two boxes filled with tubes of acrylic paint.

Pretty Boy sighed. "Thanks for thinking of us, Miss Lebrun, but we're not into the kind of art you hang on walls. Right, Tessa?"

"Percy's right." I felt like a fraud though. The closest I'd come to doing any art since getting busted in June was messing around with the cover of my journal. I'd glued a sheet of art paper on top of it, then sketched out a wreath of boxing gloves and colored them in with magic markers. The whole project had taken about half an hour.

But then my eyes landed on the tubes of acrylic paint, lined up in a neat row and sealed in shrink-wrap. I'd never been able to resist brand-new art supplies. Saturday mornings when I was growing up, Mom would ask, "If you could be anywhere in the world today, where would it be?" I could have said Paris or the North Pole, but I always came up with the same answer: the art-supply shop downtown.

Mom and I would wander up and down the aisles, and then, before we left, she'd let me choose one thing. When I was little, I'd go for paint-by-number sets—and, once, a paint-your-own-umbrella kit—but later I graduated to sketch pads, canvases and tubes of acrylic paint. Just like the ones Miss Lebrun was tempting me with now.

"Maybe," I began hesitantly, hoping Pretty Boy wouldn't get too upset over what I was about to say, "well, maybe we could try to work on some canvases. Just this once. It could be an experiment—and a way of supporting the open house. What do you say, Percy?"

"I'll think about it." It was more than I'd expected from him.

But then Pretty Boy raised his fists to his face as if he was defending himself in a fight. "And for fuck's sake, will you quit calling me, Percy?"

There was going to be a boxing demonstration at the open house. "I could use Randy and Whisky for that," Big Ron said. "If the two of you think you can behave yourselves."

"Of course we can," they said at the same time. I figured they liked the idea of showing off their boxing skills.

Big Ron also came up with the idea of offering a short, basic boxing lesson to people who wanted to try it out. "I want them to understand what it really feels like to box," he said.

The grade tens complained about getting stuck with the gruntwork. Miss Lebrun had made them responsible for cleaning up the school and organizing snacks. "No junk food!" I'd heard her warn them. "We want to send the message that we promote healthy habits here. I'm thinking apples, cheese cubes, maybe some plain popcorn. The low-sodium kind."

Jasmine and Di were handling publicity. They designed a poster of their own and plastered it all over the neighborhood.

Miss Lebrun had also warned us not to tear down any of the posters for the meeting on the Thursday night. She said that would send a bad message. "All voices deserve to be heard," she told us, "even ones we may disagree with. It's called democracy."

Pretty Boy grumbled when she said that, but he stopped tearing down the other posters.

Mr. Turner popped by more often now that we'd begun to prepare for the open house. Pretty Boy and I had decided to collaborate on one of the paintings. We wanted to try combining our two styles, and I was psyched about it. We were going to do a background of corporate logos and my trademark sign and, over that, Pretty Boy's butterfly people.

"What I like," Pretty Boy had told me, "is the juxtaposition of two worlds: the corporate world that's everywhere around us, and our inner worlds, where we're trying to become who we're meant to be."

I must've looked at him funny when he said that. "What's wrong?' he asked.

"Nothing," I said. "I just didn't know you were so deep."

Pretty Boy winked. "I told you, I like to keep a low profile."

We were sitting on the floor, prepping the canvas, when Mr. Turner walked by. "I was thinking," he said, "of some ideas for the two of you. A little inspiration, if you catch my drift."

"We've got plenty of inspiration of our own," Pretty Boy told him.

"But thanks anyhow," I added.

Mr. Turner didn't get the message. Even principals can be obtuse, I guess. "What I was thinking was maybe you could do a portrait of two boxers—a boy and a girl—shaking hands. An image like that…well, it would convey an important message and help with public relations."

"The thing is," I told Mr. Turner, "we've already come up with a plan of our own."

"The thing is," Pretty Boy added dryly, "you can't go telling artists what kind of art to make. Art is an expression of a person's soul."

Mr. Turner looked hurt. "It was just a suggestion," he said.

Pretty Boy dipped his paintbrush into the primer. "Don't worry about it," he said. "All voices deserve to be heard—even ones we disagree with."

"It's called democracy," I added.

It was pouring, so we took our break in the kitchen. The grade tens had cleaned out the refrigerator. When Pretty Boy opened it to get some apple juice, the air smelled like bleach, not moldy food. Overall, it was an improvement. We talked mostly about the open house, which was coming up in less than a week. Jasmine wondered whether the woman from next door would show up.

"Of course she'll come," Pretty Boy said. "A snoopy bitch like her won't be able to resist."

"Language, Percy!" Miss Lebrun said, raising her eyebrows.

Di didn't think the woman would turn up. "She doesn't really want to change her opinion about us."

I agreed with Di. "If she won't come to us, we should go to her," I suggested.

"What do you have in mind exactly?" Jasmine asked.

"We could go over there and personally invite her to the open house."

"Don't look at me," Pretty Boy said. "I'm not going over there."

"I wasn't looking at you," I told him. "She might remember that you gave her the finger."

"Or that he destroyed her precious sunflowers," Di said.

"Why does everyone keep pinning that on me?' Pretty Boy asked.

"You should go," Jasmine said to me. "With Randy. Just make sure *you* do the talking. The lady may not have all day."

Randy was eating an apple. "Hey," he said, "play nice."

"Playing nice," said Jasmine, "is overrated."

A half hour later, Randy and I were standing on the front porch of the house next door. "I feel like a Jehovah's Witness," I told him.

"I should've worn a suit," Randy said. I was too surprised to laugh. It was the first time I'd ever heard him crack a joke.

It was a warm day, and the living-room window was open. We could hear the whir of what sounded like a sewing machine. Then the whirring stopped and we heard a woman's voice. "You see how hard I work," she was saying. "I never even take a day off from all this damn sewing. And you know why? So you can keep going to that school! Don't you understand it's your only ticket out of this lousy neighborhood? You're staying in that school, and I don't want to hear another word about it."

Someone answered in a softer voice, but we couldn't make out the words.

Randy nudged my elbow. "Maybe we should…come back later."

I thought we should get it over with. I rang the doorbell. I had a sick feeling in the pit of my stomach.

"Get the door, will you?" we heard the woman shout. "It's probably someone who needs alterations."

I saw a finger push aside a corner of the lace curtain in the door window. Then I saw the top of a head of messy brown hair. A few seconds later, the door opened.

A boy in what looked like a private-school uniform—white shirt, navy tie, gray flannel pants—peeked out. He looked like he was around twelve, and he had his mom's dandelion hair. His eyes darted back and forth between me and Randy. "Can I help you?" he asked. At least he had better manners than his mother.

"We…uh…" I was starting to sound like Randy. "We go to the school next door, and we wondered if we might talk to your mom."

"I'm sorry," the boy said, and he looked like he meant it, "but I don't think she wants to talk to you."

"Eddie!" his mom called from the back of the house. "Who's at the door? Is it a customer?"

"Nobody!" the boy called back. "Just some kid selling chocolate bars. I told him we didn't want any."

"Well then, Eddie," I said, handing him the brochure Jasmine and Di had printed up about the open house, "could you give her this? And could you let her know we'd really like her to come to our open house next week?"

"You could come too," Randy told Eddie.

Eddie looked up at Randy. I knew he was admiring Randy's muscles. "You do boxing?" he asked in a low voice.

"Yup," Randy said.

"Can you beat someone up?"

I could see Randy considering the question. "It would depend on if I had to."

Eddie looked over his shoulder. There was no sign of his mom. "What if you had to?" he asked.

Randy grinned. "Well then I could."

Eddie shifted from one foot to the other. Then he looked at me. "Do girls box too?"

"Yup."

"Is it fun?"

Until that moment, I hadn't thought about whether boxing was fun. Mostly, when I thought about boxing, I thought about how hard it was, how tiring, and how much I still had to learn. I still had trouble remembering how to put my hand wraps on right.

"Well, is it?" the boy asked.

"Boxing's cool," I told him. And I realized I meant it.

ELEVEN

"I guess…" Randy said as we headed back to New Directions. He let his voice trail off.

"What do you guess?" A conversation with Randy required more patience than I had right then.

"I guess that didn't go too well." He sighed as if he was relieved to have got the thought out.

"It went okay. Eddie seems like a decent kid. I'll bet he gives his mother the brochure."

"She'll tear it up," Randy said.

"How do you know?"

"That's how people are." Randy paused, searching for the right words. "They make their minds up and then they won't budge."

"I hope you're wrong."

Randy stopped when we reached the sidewalk. He put his hand on my elbow, as if he wanted his touch to tell me something. "People make up their minds about me," he said finally. He didn't sound sorry for himself—more like he was reporting a fact. "They think I'm dumb. Good-looking, but dumb." Then he looked right at me. It's not easy to stay calm when a guy as hot as Randy is staring into your eyes. "Is that what you think?"

"Of course not. The dumb part, I mean."

I wondered if he could tell I was lying.

Maybe because I was so focused on Randy's hotness, I didn't notice Cyrus at first. Or maybe it was because I didn't expect Cyrus to be standing in front of New Directions. Of course, he was lugging his tripod on his back. I hadn't seen him for nearly three weeks. For a while I didn't even answer his texts or phone messages. We'd only just started talking again.

"Could you...uh, please, get your hands off my girl-friend?" Cyrus caught my eye when he said *girlfriend*. I guess he was checking to see if the term still applied. I wasn't sure if it did. I hadn't completely forgiven him after our fight at the park.

Randy let go of my elbow. "Who're you?" he asked Cyrus.

Cyrus's face was sweaty. I wondered if it was from the heat or if knowing Randy was a boxer made him nervous. Or maybe it was because Randy was hot.

"I'm Cyrus. Tessa's boyfriend." He shot me another look.

There was nothing wrong with Cyrus's build, but next to Randy he looked scrawny. Then again, most guys would look scrawny next to Randy.

"We were just talking," Randy told Cyrus. "I'm Randy." He extended his hand to shake Cyrus's.

"Tessa mentioned you." I knew Cyrus was remembering Randy's nickname. He shook Randy's hand, mostly because he had no choice. "Good to meet you, man." Then Cyrus leaned in to kiss me. I could have ducked, but I got caught up in all the things that were familiar about Cyrus—his voice, his smell, the way he ran his fingers through his curly hair when he talked. Not to mention that he'd obviously gone out of his way to come to New Directions, wanting to make up with me.

Still, when our lips met I couldn't help thinking that Cyrus was acting like a dog marking his territory. He'd basically peed on my leg. I didn't appreciate being treated like a hydrant.

Randy's phone vibrated. "Hey, babe," he said when he took the call. He walked to the corner of the yard, leaving me and Cyrus alone outside the school.

I wanted Cyrus to come in and meet the others and see the canvases Pretty Boy and I had been working on, but Cyrus said there wasn't time. "I really wish I could. Next time, okay?" He squeezed my hand. "Besides, I've got a surprise for you. We're going somewhere special."

I ran inside for my backpack. Jasmine and Di must've been watching from the window. "That your cameraman?" Di wanted to know.

"Why didn't you bring him inside?" Jasmine asked. "You afraid one of us hotties'll steal him?"

When I got back outside, Cyrus slung his arm around my waist.

When I turned to look behind me, I could see that Jasmine and Di were back in the window. I waved up at them. I hoped they thought Cyrus was cute.

He pulled me closer as we walked down the block toward the metro station. "I hope you're not giving that Randy guy the impression you're interested in him."

"I'm not interested in him. We're just friends."

Cyrus stopped walking and turned to look at me. "You sure?" I could feel him watching my face. Now he was acting like he was a lawyer and I was a witness on the stand. I didn't know what felt worse—being treated like a fire hydrant or like a criminal.

"Of course I'm sure. Don't be a jerk."

"I'm glad to hear it," he said, totally ignoring that I'd called him a jerk. Still, I hoped he'd gotten the message.

There was a green space across from the metro. It was too small to be called a park, although it had a slide and a rickety set of swings. I spotted Whisky on one of them—not swinging, just kicking the dirt under it. A guy I didn't know was with him. I was about to shout hello, but then I saw the guy hand Whisky a paper bag. When Whisky took a swig, I knew there was booze in it.

Cyrus noticed them too. He tugged on my hand. "Let's speed it up," he whispered to me. "It's a rough neighborhood."

I didn't tell him one of the guys went to New Directions. Cyrus would only use it as another argument against the school.

"So where are you taking me?" I asked when we were walking through the turnstiles at the metro station.

"Don't you want it to be a surprise?"

When we got off at Berri-UQAM and switched to the orange metro line, I guessed we were going to Chinatown. Cyrus knew I loved Chinese food.

"All right." Cyrus threw his hands up in the air. "I give up. We are going to Chinatown. But not to eat—at least, not right away. I found this guy who manages a building there. He's letting me have access to the roof." From the excited way Cyrus was speaking, I knew the arrangement he'd made had something to do with photography.

"If the weather's right on Saturday," he went on, "I'll get to spend the whole day shooting. I checked the forecast and there's supposed to be a mix of sun and cloud— not too sunny though." I knew from hanging out with Cyrus that photographers felt the same way about full sunlight as vampires did. "Wait till you see the view, Tessa. It's gonna blow you away. These are going to my best photos ever." I'd never noticed before how fast Cyrus talked. Maybe it was because I was comparing him with Randy.

I didn't say what I was thinking—that maybe he was getting a little ahead of himself here. Cyrus had arranged a photo shoot. The Magnum Photos agency hadn't phoned to sign him up.

"How'd you talk the building manager into it?" I asked when we were sitting on one of the benches, waiting for the next metro, and Cyrus finally let me get a word in.

"It helped when I mentioned I could pay him a hundred dollars for his trouble. He introduced me to the security guard who's going to let me go up to the roof."

I felt my phone vibrate in my pocket, and I took it out to check the display. It was my mom, writing to tell me she'd defrosted spaghetti sauce for supper. I texted her back to say I was with Cyrus and that we'd be eating in Chinatown.

Cyrus was leaning over my shoulder, trying to read what I was writing. I hit Send and put the phone away.

"Who was texting you?" Cyrus's tone bugged me. It sounded as if he thought he had a right to know.

"Nobody."

"You obviously weren't texting nobody. Who was it, Tessa? Was it Randy? Randy Randy?"

That made me laugh.

"Show me your phone, Tessa."

I shook my head. "Cyrus, do you have any idea how crazy you sound?"

Cyrus looked down at his sneakers, then lifted his head and looked back at me. "Maybe I am a little jealous.

It's just…you're hanging out with all these new kids…and then there's Randy…"

I knew I was Cyrus's first serious girlfriend. I just hadn't realized he was so insecure. Since getting angry didn't seem to be working, I thought I'd try a different strategy. "You need to work on your jealousy issues. Besides," I told him, "I have a thing for you. Not Randy."

Cyrus gave me a little smile. "You're right. I'll work on it." He paused. "So who were you texting?"

I almost laughed. "You call that working on your jealousy issues? It was my mom!"

"How come you won't show me your phone then?"

I pulled the phone out again and flashed it in front of Cyrus's face. "There! I'm showing it to you now, Cyrus."

I watched his eyes scan the tiny screen. It would have been a good time for him to apologize for acting like a lunatic, but he didn't.

I probably shouldn't have agreed to go with Cyrus to Chinatown. I knew we were having problems, and I didn't like him acting like he owned me, but I wasn't ready to break up with him. Maybe I liked the *idea* of Cyrus more than I actually liked *him*.

We got off at the Place d'Armes stop. I swear I could smell fried eggrolls from inside the station. When you took

the escalator up and exited on St-Laurent Boulevard, you
could have been in Hong Kong, not Montreal. Ducks with
goose-bumpy skin and long skinny necks hung upside down
in store windows. Outside, there were racks filled with
giant prickly vegetables I'd never tasted and didn't know
the names of.

Cyrus said I had to see the rooftop where he'd be doing
his photo shoot.

When we showed up, Mr. Lee, the security guard, was
in the lobby, drumming his fingers on the high desk in front
of him. He seemed glad to see us. I guess not that much
happens when you work security. "This your lady?" he asked
Cyrus. The ring of keys hanging from Mr. Lee's belt jangled
as he stepped out from behind his desk.

"My name's Tessa," I told Mr. Lee.

"You got yourself quite a boyfriend," he said. "He takes
charge. Young men like him, they go places."

I knew from the way Cyrus shifted his shoulders that he
was basking in the compliment. "Look, Mr. Lee," he said,
"I was hoping you'd let me take Tessa up to the roof. So I
could show her the view."

"Show her the view, heh? I guess that could be arranged."

Mr. Lee looked at Cyrus and Cyrus looked back at him.
I could tell they were communicating, but I didn't know
about what—until Cyrus reached into his front pocket,
where he keeps his wallet. I felt sorry for Mr. Lee when he
accepted the twenty-dollar tip Cyrus handed him.

The transaction didn't seem to bother Mr. Lee. "Go right up," he said, gesturing to the bank of elevators in the middle of the lobby.

Mr. Lee lifted his chin to the row of closed-circuit TV monitors by his desk. "I'll be keeping an eye on you two lovebirds."

We took the elevator to the tenth floor. From there, we had to take a long, narrow flight of stairs to the rooftop. I ran straight up. I'd never have been able to do that before I started training. Cyrus stopped twice to catch his breath. "Must be all this equipment I'm carrying," he said when I looked down at him from the landing.

There was a Do Not Enter sign on the door that led to the rooftop, but I pushed it open anyhow. Even ten floors up, I could smell eggrolls.

The roof's surface was covered in tar paper with gravel sprinkled over it. When we walked, our feet made crunching sounds. Someone had set out two lawn chairs. I wondered if he'd also paid for the privilege.

Cyrus took my hand and led me to the far edge. "You were right," I said. "The view's amazing." Below us, not too far in the distance, was the St. Lawrence River.

The view reminded me that Montreal was a giant island.

"Now look this way." Cyrus put his hand on my waist and turned me a little to the left.

In front of us was another building. It was about the size of the one we were in—or, in our case, on. There was nothing beautiful or remarkable about the other building. It was made of gray stone. "So?" I said to Cyrus.

"That's what I'm going to be shooting." Cyrus grinned.

"Are you telling me you spent a hundred and twenty bucks so you could photograph some old gray building?"

"Look at it, Tessa. Really look."

So I did. This time, I noticed two pigeons pecking each other on one of the windowsills.

"What do you see?" Cyrus asked.

"I see two pigeons on a windowsill."

"You're getting warmer. Tell me what else you see."

"I think I see a spider plant in another window. And a tall lamp. Cyrus, are you going to be taking photos of what you can see in that other building's windows? Is that even legal?"

Cyrus laughed. "Of course it's legal. Besides, I'm not looking for anything kinky. It's an office building, Tessa. No one'll be there over the weekend except maybe a janitor. What I'm interested in is the lonely *feeling* of an empty building—that spider plant you mentioned, the lamp, a desk with nothing on it or piled high with papers. With my tele-photo zoom, I'll be able to see inside a lot of windows."

"Hmm," I said. Maybe it wasn't such a bad idea after all.

"Of course, I'll need better light than we've got today. Hold this, will you?" Cyrus handed me his tripod. He took out his camera and started snapping photos of the building across from us.

"I thought you said the light wasn't right."

"It isn't," he said as he continued snapping. "This is just a *test shoot.*" He kneeled down to get another angle.

Because I knew this could take a while, I went to sit down on one of the lawn chairs. Sitting felt good. My muscles were sore from working out.

"Careful with my tripod!" Cyrus called out.

"I'm getting hungry," I told him.

He wasn't listening. This was one of those times that Cyrus's commitment to his photography got on my nerves.

"I'm getting hungry," I said again.

When Cyrus didn't answer, I got up from the lawn chair and walked over to the other side of the roof. From here, I could see all of Chinatown. The giant gold-and-red decorative arch on St-Laurent Boulevard, the neon restaurant signs with Chinese lettering, the square where people practiced tai chi on Sunday mornings. A garbage truck was making its rounds. A woman dragging a green garbage bag rushed to get it to the curb in time.

Photographing what was in the building across the street was a cool idea, but this view was interesting too. Being up here gave me distance, helped me see the beauty in an ordinary street scene.

The constant clicking of Cyrus's camera finally stopped. "Come look over here," I called out to him.

Cyrus came to stand behind me. He put his hand on my neck and massaged the dip between my shoulder blades.

"Don't you think this would make a good photo too?"
I asked Cyrus.

He looked out at Chinatown. I hoped he'd see what I
had. "It doesn't do much for me," he said. "Hey, where's my
tripod?"

"Relax," I told him. "It's right there. On the lawn chair."

"Okay, okay," Cyrus said. "I just got a little worried. You
know what they say about that Gitzo tripod. It's the—"

"Ferrari of tripods." It wasn't hard to finish Cyrus's
sentence. He was almost as obsessed with that tripod as he
was with his camera.

"Have a look at what I shot," Cyrus said.

Cyrus had caught the pair of pigeons. He'd also caught
a mop leaning, like a tired person, against a metal filing
cabinet. Cyrus might not be as hot as Randy, and he was
possessive and jealous and he talked a lot about himself, but
when I saw his photos, I was...well...dazzled. How could I
break up with a guy who still dazzled me?

After we left the building, we decided to get dumplings
on de la Gauchetière Street. Dumplings had two things
going for them: they were quick and cheap. The dumpling place was tiny, with a white linoleum floor. Red paper
lanterns hung over the tables. We ordered at the counter.
The door to the kitchen was open, and I could see a team of
Asian ladies in hairnets busily shaping dough.

We were standing at the counter discussing what to
order (I wanted vegetarian dumplings; Cyrus wanted the

lamb and coriander) when someone pushed open a door behind me. I stepped aside to make room.

Out came a small woman pushing a large metal bucket on wheels. The bucket was almost as big as she was. She pushed too hard, and the mud-colored water inside swished and slopped over the top. You could tell she was in a hurry.

The black nail polish and the weird haircut gave her away.

"Jasmine?" I said. "Is that you?"

"No," she answered in a voice that was so cool and dry it could only belong to her. "It isn't."

It wasn't easy to eat our dumplings with Jasmine washing the floor nearby.

Finally, she stopped washing and came over to our table. Her black nail polish was so chipped, there were more pink spots than black ones on her nails.

"Can you sit down for a few minutes?" I asked.

"No fraternizing with the customers," she said. Then she turned to Cyrus. "I just wanna know one thing. Why're you looking at me like that?"

"I ...uh...I...wasn't looking at you like anything." Cyrus sounded more like Randy by the second.

"What about you?" Jasmine looked at me. "You got a problem with me working here?"

"No, of course not. It's just..."

"Just what?"

"It's just...I heard you inherited a lot of money. You know, when your parents died. But maybe that was just gossip."

I'd never let on before that I knew Jasmine's parents were dead. I hoped she wouldn't be angry I'd mentioned it.

Jasmine dipped her mop into the gray water. "It's not gossip," she said. "I did inherit a shitload of money. But my aunt had signing privileges on my trust fund, and she helped herself to most of it. So now you know why I mop floors six days a week for minimum wage. If I save everything I earn, I'll be able to afford my own place by May."

TWELVE

I can always tell what's on my mom's mind from the library books on her night table. This week, there were three: *A Simple Plan to Help Your Teenage Vegetarian Get Enough Protein*, *The Boxing Diet* and *Moms and Daughters: How to Build Genuine Intimacy*.

She'd made red-bean burgers on whole-wheat rolls for dinner. Mom just about glowed when I asked for a second burger. Boxing makes you hungry.

I told Mom about Jasmine and her aunt. Mom was horrified. "Imagine frittering away a child's inheritance! It's immoral. Why don't you invite Jasmine over one of these nights? There's a recipe for tofu lasagna that I want to try out."

Mom and I weren't rich, but we weren't poor either. She'd worked her way up from a job as bank teller to assistant manager of a branch near our house. "Maybe we could invite the aunt too—and I could give her some pointers about handling her finances," Mom said.

I could just see Mom turning Jasmine and her aunt into a new project. "No way," I told her. "That would put Jasmine over the edge. As it is, she's already teetering."

Because we lived on a single salary, I tried not to ask for too much stuff. Mom believed that people didn't really need a lot of the stuff they bought. Most of the time, I agreed with her. A guy I knew at Tyndale collected sneakers—he had over a hundred pairs. It was obscene.

But there was one thing I wanted badly: my own boxing gloves. All of the other kids at New Directions had their own. I was still using the banged-up ones Big Ron had lent me. The stitching was coming loose, and every time I put them on, I imagined the hundreds—possibly thousands—of other sweaty hands that had been inside them.

So I brought it up after dinner. "How much are they?" Mom wanted to know.

"Fifty for the polyethylene ones. A hundred for leather. The leather ones smell amazing," I added hopefully.

Mom put one finger over her mouth the way she does when she's adding numbers in her head. "I'll give you the money for the polyethylene ones." Then she looked at me and I could tell she knew what I was thinking. "I don't want you working part-time. I want you to concentrate on school. That's what matters most. More than leather boxing gloves."

It was when we were doing the dishes that I asked Mom if she wanted to see my boxing moves.

"Sure," she said, though she didn't sound enthusiastic.

I made her sit at the kitchen table. Then I stepped back into the dining room so I'd had plenty of room and she'd have a good view.

"Here's a straight punch," I said as I demonstrated. I stepped toward her, rotating my hips with every punch and keeping my guard up. Big Ron would've been proud.

"Wanna try?" I asked Mom as I got closer.

"Boxing isn't really my thing," Mom said.

"It wasn't my thing either," I told her. "C'mon, just try a couple of moves. Here, let me show you."

Mom forgot to keep her guard up. She also forgot to rotate her hips. But even so, her punch had power. I ducked in time—otherwise she might've connected.

What I didn't expect was for Mom to laugh after she threw that punch.

I'd never heard her laugh so hard.

Soon she was out of breath—from the punching, but also probably from laughing. "It feels better than I expected," she managed to say.

Later on, when I was going to my room to study, Mom was lying on the couch, reading *The Boxing Diet*. "I'm glad about the boxing..." she said when she saw me in the hallway, looking at her.

I could tell from the way she let her voice trail off that there was more she wanted to say.

"Is it hard for you?" she asked.

"Boxing?"

"Not just the boxing." She was watching me the way I'd been watching her before. "Being around violence."

I knew she was remembering the hockey riot. It was something we never talked about. Maybe Mom figured not mentioning it would help me forget. But now I wondered if maybe I wasn't the only one who had been traumatized that night. Maybe Mom had been too. Maybe that was why she never brought it up.

"Violence still makes me feel panicky inside," I told her. "But less than before."

She adjusted her glasses. "Tess..." She stopped to take a breath. "I'm sorry about what happened the night of the..." She couldn't even say it. "I should have done a better job of protecting you."

I hoped she wasn't going to cry. In all my life, I'd never seen my mom cry. Not even that night.

"You got more banged up than I did."

"Oh, that"—Mom wiped the side of her face, the side where, if you looked closely, you could still see the faintest scar—"that looked worse than it was."

"It was my fault." I said it so quietly, I wasn't sure Mom would hear.

But she did. "Your fault? Of course it wasn't your fault. You don't really think that, do you?"

I looked down at the floor. "I let go of your hand."

"Of course you let go of my hand, Tessa. We were caught in the mob. You couldn't have held on to my hand—not with all those people."

For a second, I could feel the bodies pressing in on us the way they had that night. "Do you remember Rachel?"

"Rachel?" Mom looked puzzled.

"From camp. She was staying with her grandparents down the street—when we lived in our old apartment."

"Oh, that Rachel," Mom said. "The autistic girl. She thought the world of you."

Rachel thought the world of me? No, she didn't. Not after what I did—or didn't do.

"Why are you thinking about Rachel?"

At first, I couldn't say anything. I was remembering the YouTube clip. The girls screaming and laughing as they sent the recycling bin flying down the street. The bin crashing against a wire fence. Rachel didn't come out at first. She must have been too afraid—or too banged up. When she finally did come out, the girls recorded that part too. You could hear them jeering in the background. *Loser! Weathergirl! Retard! Hope you enjoyed the ride!* Rachel on her knees, looking dazed. One hand over her face, like she was afraid someone was going to hit her. Calling my name. *Tessa? Tessa, are you okay?*

That might have been the worst part of it. That even after everything that had happened to her, she'd been more worried about me than about herself. She'd been a better friend to me than I'd been to her.

"Tessa?"

"The other girls at camp tormented Rachel. One day, Rachel and I were walking home and they trapped us. They—" I could feel the words catching in my throat. This was the first time I'd ever spoken about the memory. "They pushed her into a recycling bin and sent it flying down the street. With Rachel inside."

Mom covered her mouth, the way Di did the morning she vomited. "Oh, Tessa," she said. "That's so awful. Did they hurt you too? Did they? Is that why you never told me?"

"They didn't hurt me." It was hard to go on, but I knew I had to tell the rest. "I ran away. But I watched it happen. More than once."

"More than once? What are you talking about, Tessa? How could you have seen something more than once?"

"One of the girls recorded the whole scene. She posted it on YouTube."

Mom groaned. "Was Rachel badly hurt?"

I shook my head. "She seemed more dazed than anything else. When she crawled out of the bin, she called for me." There, I'd said it.

"Oh, Tessa," Mom said, and I could see that she was crying. Not for me—for Rachel. I walked over to the couch and sat down next to her. Then I took her hand and squeezed it.

"I should have…"

I could feel Mom watching my lips, waiting for me to finish my sentence.

I swallowed. "I should have stood up for her."

Mom wiped her eyes. "Oh, honey, it's such a sad story. Poor, poor Rachel. You're right though—you should've stood up for her. But I guess you were too afraid." She shook her head. "If only you'd come to me before—when they first started teasing her…" I could almost see Mom's brain working, trying to envision a different outcome. One in which she could have fixed things.

How could I explain that with girls like that, Mom's involvement wouldn't have helped. It might even have made things worse. I could almost hear Angela and Megan jeering, "Tessa's such a wuss! She had to go and get her mommy to protect her!"

Mom's eyes locked on mine. "Maybe," she said gently, "it's time you forgave yourself."

I nodded. What Mom said made sense. Why didn't it make me feel better?

Maybe it was because I was still picturing the dazed look on Rachel's face when she crawled out of the bin.

"I didn't know how to protect Rachel—or myself," I said. "But now I'm learning how."

Mom's not much of a night owl. So when the phone rang a little later and one of her friends from the bank asked if she wanted to go for a drink, I never would've expected her to say yes. But she did. Well, I figured, good for her. Only it felt weird to be the one left at home, waiting.

I was in my room, reading *Death of a Salesman* for English. Man, was that ever depressing! Miss Lebrun said Willy Loman represented everyman. I sure hoped that didn't include me. Imagine working your whole life and then seeing it all fall apart.

Last year, I would have called Cyrus to discuss the play. I'd have tried to explain why I didn't trust the values I saw in the world around us—we were supposed to make successes of ourselves, but what if you did? Then what? What if, after all our hard work, we still screwed up, the way Willy Loman did?

I was lying in bed thinking all that when I heard what sounded like footsteps in the hallway inside the apartment. We lived in an old building. The noise was probably coming from the pipes.

Only then I heard it again. It was the sound of the floor-boards creaking. Our floorboards.

"Mom?" I called out. Maybe she'd forgotten something or come home early. But then I'd have heard her key in the door. And wouldn't she have called out to me when she came in? "Mom?" I called a second time. My voice was as high as a bird's.

No answer.

I heard the floorboards creak again. This time, I could feel my heart pounding in my chest. Someone was in the apartment. And it wasn't my mom. I was sure of it.

When the floorboards creaked another time, I thought my heart was going to pop out of my throat. Some maniac was about to ransack our apartment and quite possibly rape and kill or, at the least, maim me. I eyed my closet. I could try hiding in there.

Now I heard the thud of footsteps. I swear I could taste the fear at the back of my throat—dry and metallic. I was too frozen to move. The fear was paralyzing not only my body, but my brain too. ·

For some reason, I imagined saying that to Big Ron. And then I heard Big Ron's answer bellowing in my head: *The fear isn't paralyzing your body or your brain. You're letting your fear do that to you. Snap out of it, Tessa Something-or-Other. You're a boxer, aren't you?* I nodded my head the way I might've if Big Ron was in the room.

"Who is it?" I called out. Just the fact that my voice worked gave me a little more courage. Then I grabbed my cell phone from my desk. But my hands were shaking too hard for me to tap out the numbers 9-1-1. Then I started getting angry. At whoever had broken into our apartment, but also at myself, for being so afraid that I couldn't use my own cell phone.

The anger helped unfreeze the rest of me. I heard two more steps. Whoever it was was coming closer. In another minute, he could be opening the door to my bedroom. Get into boxing position—now! I told myself. Left foot at...

Then I heard a familiar whistle. "Don't go freaking out, Tessa Something-Or-Other," a voice said from the hallway.

I could feel the tension seep out of me like air from a balloon.

"You're an asshole," I told Pretty Boy, and for good measure, I threw a jab that hit him in the ribs.

Pretty Boy groaned. "Now what'd you do that for?" he asked, rubbing the spot where I'd punched him.

"That's for fucking with me. By the way, you're lucky as hell my mom's not home. She'd have had the entire police force here by now."

"I waited for her to leave."

"You *waited for her to leave?* How did you even know what she looks like?"

"In my line, you gotta do your research. I saw her drop you off the first day of school. I happened to be walking by tonight when I saw her leave the building. I figured you could use a visitor."

"Haven't you ever heard of knocking?"

Pretty Boy winked at me. "Breaking in," he said, "is way more fun. Hey, I like your pj's. They're very Zen."

I looked down at the pajamas I was wearing—they had cartoon pictures of a dog doing yoga on them. "It's not so Zen to think some nut has broken into your apartment," I told him.

"Some nut *has* broken into your apartment. So, you coming or not?"

"What are you talking about?"

"You know exactly what I'm talking about." And, of course, I did. Pretty Boy was wearing a magenta feather boa and carrying his backpack. I could hear the cans of spray paint clanking inside.

"I don't know," I told him. "I promised my mom I'd stop tagging. Not to mention that I don't want to end up in youth court."

"How could you make a promise like that? It's a stupid promise. You are a tagger, Tessa Something-or-Other. It's your calling, your *métier*."

I laughed when he called tagging my *métier*. "D'you have time for a cup of tea?" I asked him.

"I guess. Unless it's that herbal shit."

THIRTEEN

For someone so *out there*, Pretty Boy was surprisingly *in here* when it came to tea.

Our pantry had a whole shelf with just boxes of tea. "Chamomile, mint, red hibiscus..." I rattled off the names to Pretty Boy as I moved boxes out of the way so I could get to the boxes behind them. "Sleepy Time, licorice..."

"What about Red Rose?" Pretty Boy asked. "It's the only tea I drink."

I found a box of Red Rose tea at the very back of the shelf. I estimated it was about ten years old, but Pretty Boy didn't need to know that. Besides, maybe tea improved with age—like wine.

Pretty Boy was fussy about teacups too. A mug, he said, wasn't right for tea. He wanted a cup with a matching saucer.

Luckily, we had some of those. When I gave him a choice of two, he couldn't tell I was teasing.

"Delicious," he said as he sipped the tea.

I'd made myself a cup of licorice tea. "So I was in Chinatown with Cyrus yesterday and we ran into Jasmine," I told Pretty Boy.

"Cyrus? I thought you dumped that pretentious jerk-off. I'd put my money on you and Randy. He's smarter than he looks."

I ignored that comment. "Cyrus and I have been having some problems. But hey, thanks for your opinion." I hoped that would shut him down. "Did you know she works mopping floors in Chinatown?"

"Of course I know. Everybody knows."

"She told me how her aunt got hold of the inheritance money," I said.

Pretty Boy took another sip of tea. "The aunt didn't just get hold of it. She gambled it away. She's hooked on black-jack. Unfortunately, she isn't any good at it."

"You're kidding," I said. I'd heard about gambling addictions, but I'd never known anyone who had one.

"I wish I was."

After that, we just sat there for a while. Then Pretty Boy went to the sink and washed out his teacup. "If we were different sorts of people, Tessa Something-or-Other, we could sit here all night and shoot the breeze, but you and I have got ourselves a meet and greet with some bare walls on de Maisonneuve. You coming or what?"

My plan was just to keep Pretty Boy company, but something about the rattle of the cans in his backpack, and the quiet streets with only the streetlamps for light, brought back the old urge to tag. In fact, I was starting to think I'd never really lost the urge—just buried it temporarily.

Pretty Boy must've known what was going through my mind. "I don't care what Miss Lebrun thinks. A piece of canvas doesn't do it for me. The streets..." He looked around him, then up at the stars. "They're alive."

De Maisonneuve Boulevard was so quiet, it felt eerie. We were nearing the part of the street that was mostly industrial. Except for one new condo, everything else was a business—a car wash, a plumbing-supply center and a handful of auto-body shops.

Pretty Boy and I spotted the bare concrete wall at the same moment. The last time I'd been in the area, I'd noticed a huge black tag on this wall. Someone must've paid to have it removed. I couldn't blame them. That tag was butt ugly. I didn't believe in tagging for the sake of tagging. In my opinion, a good tag was a work of art. I knew Pretty Boy shared my philosophy. Too bad the rest of the world didn't feel that way.

He looked at me and grinned. "What do you say we leave our mark right here? Only we make it so beautiful, no one'll make an emergency call to Graffiti MD." Graffiti MD was the name of a local cleaning service that specialized in removing tags and graffiti. Over the summer, I'd seen their trucks making the rounds.

I stepped closer to the curb. "You go ahead," I told Pretty Boy. "I'll watch for cops."

Pretty Boy stuck out his butt and did his little dance, complete with clucking sounds.

"I'm not chicken," I told him. "I'm just being careful."

Pretty Boy kept clucking. "You're chicken," he said. "You're afraid. I can smell it. You reek of fear, Tessa Something-or-Other."

"Fuck you, Pretty Boy."

Pretty Boy grinned again. "That's more like it. Come on, let's do this." I think he knew before I did that I was about to start tagging again.

We took the spray cans out of Pretty Boy's backpack. A train came by and then a lone cyclist. Otherwise we had the street to ourselves.

We started at opposite ends of the wall. I surveyed my side, mapping things out in my head, choosing the best spot for my trademark sign. Maybe tonight I'd do it on an angle, just to shake things up.

Pretty Boy didn't work with a plan. I could already hear the whoosh of spray paint as he began applying the color. "You doing your usual?" Pretty Boy's voice echoed in the dark.

"Uh-huh."

"Why don't you try something different—for a change?" he asked.

"It's my trademark, my signature," I told him. "Like butterfly people are for you."

"Who said I was doing a butterfly person?"

"You mean you're not?"

"I'm not. Artists need to change things up. Keep it fresh. Otherwise they get lazy."

"What about Salvador Dali and his melting clocks?" I knew Salvador Dalí was one of Pretty Boy's idols, even if he'd painted on canvas.

"He painted lots of other stuff besides melting clocks."

So I decided to try working Pretty Boy-style. Without a plan. I wouldn't even use black spray paint the way I'd always done. I reached for one of Pretty Boy's cans. I didn't even know what color it was until I looked at the plastic top. Forest green.

I pressed down on the nozzle, and this time, I let the jet of paint lead me. It didn't take long for me to see where I was going. I was painting a path through a forest of tall, spiky pine trees. And then, just like that, my path changed direction, leading me around a concrete corner so that I found myself on the other side of the wall. The concept was cool—if I said so myself.

I worked quickly, intensely, practically without thinking. I added branches to the pine trees and, overhead, a pair of red boxing gloves, hanging in the air like a moon.

I'd lost track of time before while I was tagging, but this was different. This time, I was following the paint and the path. I liked how it felt: free.

But when I stepped back to see from a distance what I'd done, I only saw flaws. The spots where the paint was too thick and dribbling down the concrete, or where it was too thin and wispy. The thumb on one of the boxing gloves was too fat. Maybe I needed some black after all.

I looked over at Pretty Boy's side. I remembered the first time I'd met him—before I knew what his name was—and how he must've felt me watching him then too.

He hadn't painted a butterfly person. But he'd stayed on theme. Pretty Boy's side of the wall had been taken over by a giant, bulbous larva. Butterflies, caterpillars, larvae—the connection was obvious. But what made Pretty Boy's larva special was that it was melting.

"I like it," I told him.

Pretty Boy liked mine too, though his reaction was more low-key. "Nice," he said. "I like how you used two sides of the wall."

We could hear the rumble of a car coming down Wilson Avenue. Was it the cops? I could feel my heartbeat quickening. Why had I let Pretty Boy talk me into this? My mom would kill me if I got caught tagging again! I'd get kicked out of New Directions and end up a high-school dropout. And what if I got sent to youth court?

We tossed the cans into Pretty Boy's backpack. Then he put his arm through mine, bringing me in close. Soon we were strolling down the sidewalk along de Maisonneuve. If it weren't for Pretty Boy's feather boa, we might've been any couple out for a late-night walk.

The rumble got louder as the car approached us. It wasn't a cop car. It was a souped-up old black Mustang with silver hubcaps that gleamed in the dark. "Shit," Pretty Boy muttered when the car slowed down.

There were three guys inside.

"D'you know them?" I whispered.

"You could say that."

The guy sitting in the front passenger seat rolled down his window and stuck his head out. "Hey, Percy," he said, "we've been driving around looking for you all night. How come you're not picking up your phone?"

The guy was bigger than Pretty Boy, but he had his fine features and the same lilt when he spoke. So this was one of the brothers Jasmine had told me about.

"I turned my phone off because I wanted to be left alone," Pretty Boy said.

Now the guy sitting in the backseat rolled down his window and joined the conversation. He looked so much like the brother in the passenger seat, I wondered if they were twins. "You got yourself a lady, Pretty Boy? I thought you didn't swing that way."

Pretty Boy pulled me in a little closer. We were speed-walking now. The old me would've had trouble keeping up.

The car pulled in so close to the sidewalk, the front tire skimmed the curb. "You have to come with us, Percy," the passenger-seat brother said. His voice, which had been playful before, now sounded serious—and impatient.

"I don't *have* to do anything, Rufus," Pretty Boy said.

"We could drive your girlfriend home. Then we got something special for you," Rufus said.

"I don't want your something special." I felt the muscles in Pretty Boy's arm pop up. I hoped he wasn't planning to punch anyone out.

"It's top-quality Jamaican ganja, mahhn." The backseat brother's imitation of a Rastafarian was terrible.

"You know I'm done with that shit, Anthony," Pretty Boy said.

"You're never done with that shit," Anthony called out.

"I'm telling you, I'm done." Pretty Boy was shouting. "I don't want to go to juvie again. Now back off, will ya?" The muscles in Pretty Boy's arms were twitching now.

"Let him walk his girlfriend home," I heard Anthony say in the backseat. "Maybe he's finally gonna get himself laid. We gotta scope out the neighborhood anyhow." Then he shouted, "Just make sure you answer your phone next time we call, little brother! You help us out, and we got some top-quality ganja with your name on it. You smoke a little o' that and you'll quit whining about juvie."

"Let's go," I heard the driver tell Rufus and Anthony. They rolled up their windows, and the tires squealed as the car took off.

That's when Pretty Boy did something I'd never heard him do. He sighed. A deep, really relieved sigh. I hadn't realized till then how much his brothers freaked him out.

FOURTEEN

The grade tens hadn't only looked after refreshments. They'd also turned a white bedsheet into a colorful banner and hung it outside the school. Technically, the banner should have been classified as décor, which wasn't their responsibility, but Pretty Boy and I decided not to mention it. "Nobody knows better than us," I told Pretty Boy while struggling to keep a straight face, "how important it is to encourage creativity in troubled teens."

But at four o'clock on the day of our open house, the banner had to come down. Someone—we were pretty sure who—had telephoned the borough office to complain. Apparently, a school had to have a permit to display a banner, and we hadn't applied for one. So much for creativity.

I needed to put some finishing touches on our fourth canvas. I hauled it to the classroom, not expecting to find Randy and Di huddled at the back of the room. Di was blowing her nose. Ruger was sitting on the floor next to her, his dark eyes alert and focused on his owner.

It was too late for me to turn around. They'd already seen me, and they couldn't have missed the canvas, which was halfway into the room.

Ruger's ears pricked up when Randy sprung from his chair. I'd never get over how much quicker Randy was with movement than with words.

"Let me help with that, Tessa," he said, taking hold of one end of the canvas and lifting it through the air as if it were made of feathers.

"I didn't realize you were in here. I could go work someplace else." To be honest, I had no idea where else to go. The kitchen wasn't big enough, and there was no way I could drag the canvas downstairs to the gym.

Randy shot a look at Di as if he was clearing things with her.

Di took a fresh Kleenex from her handbag and blew her nose again. "It's okay," she said. "I don't have any secrets from Tessa." Ruger flopped down on the floor, frog-style, without lifting his eyes off Di.

I set up at the front of the room, and Randy went back to his chair. I tried not to listen in on the conversation.

Only it was hard not to. They didn't even bother trying to lower their voices.

"I'm just telling you what"—Randy struggled to get his sentence out—"what I know about Sal and what I know about guys."

"You don't understand. It's not like that with me and Sal. He loves me. I know he does." I could tell Di was trying to convince herself.

Afterward, I wondered why Randy didn't just give up then. Why not let Di go on believing that Sal loved her? He must've thought he really needed to make his point. He must've thought it could help Di—even if it hurt her right then.

"You don't know Sal like I do." I was surprised when Randy's voice broke. I hadn't expected him to get so emotional. "If you think I'm a dog around the ladies"— Ruger looked up when he heard the word *dog*—"and I'm not saying I'm not, Sal…Sal's way worse. There's something else I got to tell you. Sal's got…he's got somebody else." Randy fell silent. He'd said what he had to.

Di was tearing up. Ruger's brindled ears went back, attentive.

Di made gulping sounds. "How do you know?" she asked Randy.

"I've seen them together."

"So big deal. You saw Sal with some other chick. He hangs out with lots of chicks."

"They were...doing more than hanging out." Randy paused, and this time, I didn't think it was because he was having trouble finding his words. "Sal got that other chick pregnant too."

"No way! You're lying!" Di was shouting now. A low rumble came from Ruger.

Randy ignored the dog. He went over to Di and put his hand on her shoulder. "I'm not lying. You just don't want to hear it."

Next thing I knew, Di was crumpled like some wad of paper on the floor. Ruger was licking her face and whimpering. Di tried pushing him away, but the dog wouldn't go. I'd never heard anyone sob the way Di was sobbing now. It was if she was trying to swallow back her tears so no one would hear her. But that only made her choke.

Randy shifted from one foot to another. "Take it easy, Di," he kept saying. Only that made things worse.

I couldn't paint—I couldn't even pretend to paint. Not with Di sobbing like that. I just wasn't sure I knew her well enough to intervene.

In the end, I went over for Randy as much as for Di. He looked trapped—like a butterfly between two panes of glass.

"You said what you needed to," I told him, swatting his arm. "Now get lost, will you?"

Randy flew for the door. Before he reached it, he turned and started sputtering an apology. "Look, I'm sorry, Di. But you needed to know."

I put my arm around Di's shoulders. "Everything'll be okay," I said, not because I thought so but because I couldn't think of what else to say.

"He hasn't called me in three weeks," Di blurted out between sobs. "Randy says Sal's got some other chick pregnant too. How could he do that to me? To us?"

I wanted to say Sal was an irresponsible jerk, that she was better off without him, that he'd have made a terrible father, but I knew that wasn't what Di wanted to hear. So I came up with something else. "It's not about Sal anymore. It's about you, Di, and what you decide to do about"—I paused to find the right word—"your future."

"I'm not getting an abortion, if that's what you mean." Di's eyes were shining. I thought the shine came from a combination of tears and willpower.

"I didn't mean that," I said. "But having a baby when you're sixteen—well, it's gotta be hard."

"I'll be seventeen by the time the baby comes." Talking about the baby seemed to calm her down.

I looked at Di's belly. Even though she still wasn't showing, it was pretty amazing to imagine there was a baby growing in there. A baby with tiny fingers and toes, a baby that would grow up to be as big as any of us. I wondered if it would look like Di. "I bet it'll be a beautiful baby," I whispered.

It was one thing for Di to go on with the pregnancy, but I wondered if she was planning to keep the baby and raise it herself. I knew there were a lot of families that wanted to adopt babies. Maybe Di would find one of those families for her baby. But I worried that if I raised the possibility, Di might punch me.

Di seemed to know what I was thinking. She caressed her belly gently, as if she was caressing the baby inside. "I'm not giving my baby away either," she said.

"I never said you should."

"I could never do that." Di's eyes pooled up with tears. "That's what my parents did. That's how I ended up in foster care."

"You're in the foster system?" It probably wasn't the best question, but it popped out. She'd never mentioned it before. Maybe that was why Di cried the way she did. Maybe a kid in the foster system learned to make as little noise as possible.

"Yeah," Di said. "Why are you looking at me like that?"

"I'm not looking at you like anything."

"Let me tell you something, Tessa. The foster home I live in sucks. But it's a big improvement over the ones I was in before. You know what I've learned?" Di sounded angry.

I shook my head.

"I learned you gotta make your own family." Di turned to look around the classroom, then out at the hallway. "This place. The people in it. You're my family."

FIFTEEN

On the night of the open house, New Directions was so crowded it felt more like a bus station than a school.

I recognized some of the visitors from the neighborhood. A couple who lived up the street and grew tomatoes in their tiny front garden. An elderly woman I'd seen out with a wobbly shopping cart. A man wearing a beret. I'd noticed him a couple of streets over, walking his cat on a leash. (It's hard *not* to notice someone walking a cat on a leash.) A young couple with two kids, both wearing *Cat in the Hat* T-shirts. Some teenagers I'd seen smoking outside the metro station.

Some of our parents had come too. Mom was there, and I appreciated how she was giving me my space. She'd squeezed my hand when she first saw me, not hugged or kissed me in an embarrassing way. I'd introduced her to Miss Lebrun, who was sitting behind her desk next to Mr. Turner. The two of them were handing out brochures and talking about academics at the school. "We have a very high success rate," I heard Mr. Turner say.

At first, I worried Mom wouldn't have anyone to talk to, but when I spotted her next, she was talking to a couple who seemed about her age. The man was tall and distinguished-looking. There was a little gray at his temples, but when he laughed, his face turned boyish. The woman looked like a model in a Ralph Lauren ad—pretty without trying to be. They didn't look like they belonged at New Directions. Then again, neither did Mom.

Randy tapped my elbow. By now, I recognized his touch. It was just the right combination of soft and strong. He was wearing boxing shorts and a mesh singlet that showed off his biceps.

"Aren't you supposed to be downstairs, getting ready to spar?" I asked him.

"I...uh...came to get some ice for my water bottle. Hey"—for a second, his fingertips grazed my elbow, making it hard for me to think—"thanks for talking to Di. You were good with her."

We both looked over at Di and Jasmine. They were standing in the hallway, greeting people as they walked in and handing out the program for the evening. Di was wearing her peasant blouse. Her face was glowing.

You'd never guess that a few hours earlier, she'd been crumpled up on the floor, sobbing.

"No problem," I said to Randy. "You were good with her too. It couldn't have been easy telling her all that. Sal sounds like a total asshole. What I don't get is why girls fall for guys like him."

Randy shrugged. "Beats me. Some girls are weird that way."

"Speaking of weird girls, I don't see your fan club."

"Fan club?" But I could tell from the way he tried not to smile that he knew what I meant. He waved the back of his hand in the air. "Oh, them," he said. "I didn't tell them... about the open house. They're just a bunch of silly girls."

"Hey, good luck later. Where's Whisky anyway? I haven't seen him."

"He phoned Big Ron to say he was on his way." Randy looked away a moment. Was he worried Whisky might show up drunk? I decided it was better not to ask.

"Your parents coming?" I asked instead.

"They're here," Randy said. "Talking to that nice-looking older lady in the stripes."

"You're kidding. Those are your parents?"

"Uh-huh, but do me a favor...don't tell anyone."

"Your secret's safe with me. About that nice-looking older lady in the stripes—she's my mom. So how come you don't want anyone to know they're your parents? They seem perfectly respectable. Don't tell me they have a cat they walk on a leash."

Randy laughed. He must have recognized the guy with the beret too.

Randy's mom waved at him from across the room.

Randy waved back, but only a small wave, like the Queen of England in her limo. "She's a...doctor," Randy said. "So's my dad. What'd you call them? Respectable? It's a good word. They don't drink. They don't beat me up or steal my money. You're right. They're respectable."

It was the longest speech I'd ever heard Randy make.

Across the room, my mom was smiling at something Randy's mom had said. My mom could be annoying, but she also didn't drink or beat me or steal my money. She also never put me in foster care. "My mom's like that too," I told Randy. "Respectable. I guess we're lucky."

"We *are* lucky." Randy smiled into my eyes, and I wondered if he was flirting with me. "But I wouldn't go advertising it. Not around here."

I knew what he meant. At New Directions, having respectable parents was like a lunar meteorite—one of the most rare rocks on Earth.

Mr. Turner clapped to get everyone's attention, but there was so much talking, no one heard him. So Randy stuck two fingers in his mouth and whistled. Then he called out, "Yo!" and the whole first floor of New Directions got so quiet, you'd think we were writing a math exam.

Mr. Turner took a bow. Apparently, he didn't realize how dorky that looked. "I want to welcome you all to

New Directions. We appreciate that you've come to show your support."

Which made me wonder if anyone there had really come to show support. Were there spies for the neighborhood group in the room too? I had a feeling there probably were.

After Mr. Turner's short welcome, everyone headed down to the gym. There were so many people, I could hardly breathe going down the staircase.

Randy and Whisky were sitting side by side on a bench. Big Ron gestured for everyone to come in. He'd set up folding chairs in front of the boxing ring. There weren't enough chairs, so some people had to stand. When Di yawned several times in a row, a man offered her his seat.

I wasn't surprised when Big Ron wanted to say a few words too. "People around here," he began, "call me Big Ron—for obvious reasons." There was some uncomfortable laughter when he said that. "I want to clear up a misconception about boxing. Most people think boxing is about violence. What they don't understand is, there's a big difference between raging violence and competitive, controlled violence.

"When I was a young man, many moons ago"—again, there was some laughter from the audience—"you know who taught boxing to guys like me? Cops." Big Ron paused to let the audience absorb this information "…and priests." He paused again. "I kid you not. You know what those cops and priests understood? That young people need to channel their aggression, and boxing is a good way to do that. Which is why, tonight, I'm going to be offering a series of five-minute boxing lessons. I want you people to get a feel for what it's like to box. So you can be a better judge of what's going on here at New Directions."

Someone in the audience clapped. Someone else said, "I'd never do it. Never."

Big Ron asked everyone interested in a mini-lesson to form a line. In no time, he had about a dozen people. The first was the man with the beret. I thought Big Ron would start the guy in front of the mirrored wall, the way he'd started us, but I guess he was looking to make a more dramatic impression. He handed the guy a pair of boxing gloves and brought him over to one of the punching bags.

"I'm gonna teach you a straight punch," Big Ron told the guy. "You need to make a good fist. And don't go hitting the bag too hard."

Big Ron watched as the guy swung at the bag. On his first try, his beret went flying off his head. I tried not to laugh.

When the guy looked over at his beret, Big Ron told him not to bother with it. "You don't need a fancy hat like that in my gym. Okay, so you're gonna throw with your left hand, then your right. And I'm gonna count. You ready?"

The guy nodded. I wondered if he was already too winded to talk.

"One!" Big Ron called.

Bam, bam, bam.

I'd only been boxing since the end of August. When had the sound of punching stopped bothering me?

The guy made it to ten. Then Big Ron made him do a second set of ten straight punches, this time without stopping. By the time the guy got to four, there were giant sweat stains on his T-shirt. I guessed walking his cat wasn't giving him much of an aerobic workout. The guy slumped over when he was done.

"So tell me something—how do you feel now?" Big Ron asked him. Big Ron turned around. I knew it was because he wanted to make sure he had an audience.

One of the grade tens handed the guy a water bottle. The guy opened it and took a long swig. "I feel," the guy said, "like I have nothing left. I'm weak as a kitten."

I figured if he was using a cat simile, it was probably a good sign.

Jasmine had come to stand next to me. "Do you think he's got his cat outside, tied to a fire hydrant?" I asked her.

"Probably. Let's just hope Ruger doesn't find out. He'd chase that cat across the Metropolitan Highway."

Ruger was at the open house too. Big Ron had tried to get Di to leave the dog at the foster home, but she said she couldn't. When Di told him it was because Ruger had "abandonment issues," Big Ron had laughed and asked, "You sure you're not talking about yourself, Lady Di?"

I didn't see the woman from next door come in. I only spotted her when Big Ron was about halfway through the lineup of people who wanted to box. Because I figured I should do my bit for public relations, I went over and introduced myself. "Hi," I said, reaching out to shake her hand. "I'm Tessa McPhail. We've met before."

Her fingers felt rough, maybe from the sewing. She could've told me her name then, but she didn't. Maybe she was still miffed about her sunflowers.

"I thought Eddie might want to come tonight."

Her eyes—they were a steely gray—met mine. "How do you know my son's name?"

I decided not to say that Randy and I had already met Eddie. "I've heard you call for him. Sound really travels around here…"

She shook her head. "Tell me about it. I work from home. Sometimes you kids make such a racket, I can't sew straight. Eddie's at his study group. He goes to St. William's." She straightened her back when she said the school name.

"Thanks for coming tonight," I said.

I was congratulating myself on having successfully chatted up Eddie's mother when I heard a shriek. She had gone and opened the door to Big Ron's office—probably snooping, or maybe she thought it was the washroom, or who knows why—and seen Ruger. "Oh my god, that pit bull—it's in here. Those dogs are killers!"

Di came running over. "Ruger's the sweetest dog you'll ever meet," she said. I was hoping no one would ask how Ruger got his name.

Big Ron came to see what the fuss was about. "Ruger's a good dog, ma'am. In fact, most people want to eat *him* up." Big Ron chuckled at his own joke. The woman didn't.

Big Ron tapped Di on the arm. "Why don't you get Ruger to sing?" he asked her.

Di had been scratching Ruger behind the ears. "I love you, Ruger," she crooned.

Ruger looked up at Di and started making noises that sounded a lot like "I love you."

Some of the visitors laughed and a few others clapped. "I didn't know dogs could do that," someone said.

Big Ron took the woman from next door by the arm. "I want to show you a few boxing moves," he told her. "If you don't mind my saying so, I think boxing might help you relax."

"I don't need your help relaxing," the woman snapped.

"I certainly didn't mean to offend you, ma'am. Why don't we start this conversation over and you tell me your name?"

She didn't seem to know what to make of Big Ron—or at least, she couldn't find a way to escape his bear-paw hold. "My name's Florence," she said, a little breathlessly. "But I'm not the least bit interested in learning to box."

Big Ron's belly quaked when he laughed. "Never say never," he told her. He was still holding on to her arm.

"Florence, you say? I guess the name has something to do with flowers, right? Or *fleurs* in French. You know, Florence, you remind me of a flower. A nice-looking flower, the kind that smells good, like a rose, but has a few prickles."

I thought the part about the prickles might upset Florence, but she seemed okay with it. Or else she was just overwhelmed by Big Ron.

"Let me guess, Florence," Big Ron was saying. "You spend your days hunched over, don't you? At a computer, maybe? I can see it in your posture. You need to straighten your spine. Like this…"

Di was getting Ruger to do more tricks for the small group crowded inside Big Ron's office. Ruger sat up and held up a paw on command.

"You should bring Ruger upstairs and show them how he can open the fridge and take out a beer," Jasmine called out.

Unfortunately, that set Florence off all over again. "Alcoholic beverages on school property? I'm sure that's against the regulations."

Big Ron didn't seem too worried. "Jabbin' Jasmine's just yanking your chain, Florence," he told her. "Besides, the world's going to look different to you after you've thrown a couple of punches. Here, let me show you a couple of basic moves. Like I said, straighten your spine. Now bring in your shoulders."

Big Ron rotated his hips and threw a straight punch. Then he made Florence put her purse on the floor and do the same thing.

"A little stiff," he said as he watched her, "but not bad, not bad at all."

Florence didn't crack a smile. She was not, I decided, the smiling type.

SIXTEEN

Between the mini-lessons and the sparring demonstration, there were refreshments. It had been Miss Lebrun's idea for the grade tens to dress in white shirts and black pants. Now, looking more like servers in some dinner club than troubled teens, they circulated with trays of food. There were fruit kebabs—cubes of mango, melon and pineapple on skewers—and rolled-up cheese slices. There was also a tray of Miss Lebrun's chocolate banana bread. Big Ron grabbed two slices.

He was chomping down on his second slice when I saw him go over to Randy and Whisky. He plopped down on the bench between them, draping his huge arms around their shoulders. "I just want to have a quick word with you two before you start sparring," I heard him say.

Pretty Boy nudged me. "Quick word?" he whispered. "Big Ron? I don't think so."

I bit down on my lip so I wouldn't laugh.

Big Ron lowered his voice, but Pretty Boy and I were close enough to overhear what he was saying. "I'm counting on you guys to behave yourselves tonight. I know you have your issues, but I'm expecting you to put your differences aside and act professional. It's really important to make a good impression. And I don't want you to forget that whatever you do, you're representing our sport and this school. Do we have ourselves a deal?"

"Deal," Randy said.

"No problem," Whisky added.

Pretty Boy's phone vibrated. He walked to the corner of the room to take the call. "I gotta go take care of something," he announced when he came back.

"Are you saying you can't stay to watch them spar?"

"That's exactly what I'm saying. Takes notes for me, will ya?"

"All right then, ladies and gents," Big Ron said when he got up from the bench. "Now we're going to show you what sparring looks like. As you can see, our two boxers here are wearing protective headgear and also bigger gloves than the kind used during competitive matches." Big Ron sounded like one of those guys who narrates documentaries on the nature channel. "That's because the goal isn't for them to hurt each other, but to improve their skills—and prepare them for competition.

"They're not looking to knock each other out tonight"—Big Ron's voice was stern when he said that, and I knew the message was intended for Whisky and Randy—"but I want to warn members of the audience that boxing is a contact sport. A boxer doesn't just need to learn how to punch; he needs to learn how to take punches too." He paused for a few seconds after that, the way he did when he thought something he'd said was really brilliant and people needed time to let his brilliance sink in.

"Now, without further ado, I want you all to meet two of my finest boxers. In the red corner"—he pointed to the far end of the boxing ring—"we've got Randy Randy. He's not only a hit with the ladies, he's also one helluva boxer."

Randy raised his arm over his head to signal the crowd. There was some polite clapping.

"And in the blue corner"—Big Ron gestured toward the other end of the ring—"is Whisky. Now, I don't want you people getting the wrong impression. Whisky's only a nickname. But like the finest single malt, this here Whisky is smooth and strong."

Whisky grinned as he took a bow—and the audience clapped some more.

Big Ron waddled over to the timer, a small box with lights on it. The green light meant go, the red meant stop, and the orange light, which was accompanied by a sharp whistle, meant there were thirty seconds left in the round.

"The way this works," he told the audience, "is we're gonna have three three-minute rounds. After each round, there'll be a one-minute break. All right then, here goes." Big Ron switched on the timer.

The sparring was friendly—at least, at first.

Over and over again, Randy danced out of Whisky's path. He also showed off his combinations. Two straight punches, a quick left hook, then uppercuts—all followed by more fancy footwork.

What Whisky had going for him was power. He used one power punch after another, loading up for each one so that all his body weight was behind his punches.

As he ducked and weaved, Randy's breathing got heavier, but Whisky just kept punching. With every punch, he moved in a little closer on Randy.

I never knew three minutes could last so long. I couldn't imagine what it must've felt like for Randy and Whisky. Sweat dripped from their faces, landing like heavy raindrops on the mats.

A man came into the gym and lurched toward the ropes. "Hey, watch yourself," someone said. "That's my foot you just stepped on."

It wasn't like Whisky to drop his hands, but he did. Just like that.

Something had distracted him.

Randy took advantage, throwing two quick straight punches and hitting Whisky in the jaw. Whisky bit down hard on his lower lip.

He'd stopped to look at the latecomer. Now I looked too. The man had a craggier, lined version of Whisky's face. The smell of tobacco clung to his clothes. I knew instantly he was Whisky's father. When he grabbed the ropes, Big Ron told him to step away.

Whisky's dad lost his footing, and someone nearby managed to break his fall. He stumbled back to his feet. Even from the other side of the ring, I could smell the sharp fumes of alcohol wafting through the air like cheap cologne.

I was glad when the light finally turned red. Randy needed to catch his breath. Whisky needed to focus.

A minute later, Whisky had regained his focus—and then some. He was punching harder now than he had in the first round. Randy would have to pick up his speed if he wanted to keep dancing out of Whisky's reach.

Whisky started by taking a few straight jabs at Randy. Randy's dancing had slowed down, and this time Whisky managed to punch him in the cheek. Randy's cheekbone swelled up like a rose. Just a few seconds later, Whisky threw a left hook, slamming Randy's rib cage. Randy winced, and I swear I felt it in my chest. It was as if Whisky had slammed me too.

The green light on the timer turned to orange, and the whistle sounded. Thank God, I thought. Only thirty seconds left in round two. Randy wouldn't be able to take much more.

"Don't go so hard," I heard Big Ron hiss at Whisky. "Don't forget we got people here."

But Whisky had clearly forgotten.

When the bell sounded for the third and final round, Randy and Whisky came out from their corners. Whisky raised his glove—an indication that he wanted to touch gloves with Randy. In boxing, touching gloves is a sign of respect, a way of telling your opponent everything is cool, that despite how hard you've been going at each other, you're still friends. I knew it was Whisky's way of apologizing for what had happened in the second round. He'd lost control, and now he wanted to make things right with Randy.

I watched Randy's eyes as their gloves touched. They were flat, like pools of water on a windless day. Whisky lowered his hand. He must have assumed that by touching gloves, he'd made everything right with Randy.

I hadn't been taking boxing lessons for long, but I knew the unwritten rule that applied here. After two boxers touched gloves, there was a short grace period. They gave each other a few seconds to set up.

Randy flouted that rule.

He'd touched gloves with his left hand, but instead of giving Whisky a few seconds' grace, Randy threw a hard—a really hard—straight right-hand punch. It hit Whisky across the nose. I brought one hand to my own nose, as if it needed protection too.

Looking back, I don't remember what came first—the squirt of blood or the sound of cracking bone.

I'd never heard bone crack before, but I knew that as long as I lived, I'd never forget the sound—a crunching like what happens when you're walking on ice and it cracks. Only louder.

The blood streamed from Whisky's nose, down his chin and onto the mat. There was even blood on the ropes. Later, I wondered how it got there.

Florence covered her eyes, then uncovered them. "If this doesn't prove these kids are dangerous, I don't know what does," she said to the person sitting next to her.

Big Ron moved as if he had wings. Whisky was still standing, but he was wobbly and his eyes looked dazed, as if he was just waking up—or just falling asleep. Big Ron perched at Whisky's side, and I watched—in horror and in fascination—as Big Ron laid two fat thumbs on either side of Whisky's nose. There was a loud *pop* and then Whisky moaned.

Big Ron had popped Whisky's nose back into place, but he still had work to do. I was surprised by how gentle his movements were as he helped Whisky back to the bench.

"Get me my first-aid kit," Big Ron called. Jasmine was closest to the kit, so she grabbed it and threw it over to Big Ron.

Randy's parents had rushed over too. His mom checked Whisky's eyes and took his pulse. I watched, relieved, as she nodded to her husband to indicate that everything seemed to be okay.

Big Ron fished a roll of gauze out of his first-aid kit. Randy's dad stuffed the gauze inside Whisky's nostrils. That was when I turned away. If I hadn't, I'm pretty sure I'd have puked.

The crowd had fallen eerily silent—except for Whisky's dad. He was pushing his way to the benches, not caring if he elbowed someone or squashed their toes. "Let me sh-sh-ee my son," he said.

Miss Lebrun intercepted him. "Your son's going to be fine," she told him. "What you need right now is a cup of coffee." She took his arm and led him away from the benches.

"You sh-shure about my boy?" Whisky's dad asked. "Hey, lady, I don't want your coffee. But I could sure use a smoke."

Now that Randy's parents were attending to Whisky, Big Ron stood up to address the crowd. "Ladies and gentlemen," he said, "what you just witnessed was an unfortunate incident. One of my fighters was a little"—Big Ron paused to find the right word—"unsportsmanslike."

Florence snorted loudly. "Unsportsmanslike?" she called out. "Bloodthirsty is more like it!"

"Unsportsmanlike," Big Ron said again, drawing out each syllable of the word. Big Ron didn't look at either Florence or Randy. He didn't have to. Florence had settled back into her seat. Randy was still standing in the ring, his eyes flitting between the floor mats and the bench where Whisky was sitting.

"I want to make it clear," Big Ron continued, "that what you saw just now isn't what boxing is about. My boxers aren't perfect." Big Ron looked at the crowd, and for a moment I felt like I was in church, not in Big Ron's gym. Big Ron turned his head slowly, trying to make eye contact with as many people as possible. He stopped when he got to Florence. Then he did something that surprised me. He smiled at her. A warm, understanding smile, as if they were old friends. There was nothing fake about Big Ron's smile. He had as much reason as any of us to dislike Florence, but he didn't.

"Let me ask you something. Any of you people happen to be perfect?" Then he patted his belly. "Look at me," he said, "I sure ain't."

I knew that after everyone went back upstairs, Randy would get a lecture from Big Ron and it wouldn't be fun— or short. I also knew Big Ron would make Randy apologize.

Randy didn't need the lecture though. When he cleared his throat, everyone turned to look at him. For once, he didn't have to struggle to find his words. "I just want to tell you all I'm sorry. Really, really sorry."

Big Ron didn't think Whisky should go to the hospital. "A little bump on that nose of yours'll give you character," he told Whisky.

Whisky didn't want to go to the hospital either. He was more concerned about his dad getting home okay.

But Randy's parents insisted on taking Whisky to the hospital for an X-ray. They made Randy come too.

Later, I heard from Randy that the four of them had to wait for nearly three hours for the X-ray. At first, Whisky refused to talk to Randy. Randy even went to the hospital cafeteria to get him a milkshake, but Whisky wouldn't drink it.

Then Randy got a better idea. He went to the newsstand and found a copy of *The Ring*, a glossy boxing magazine. That turned out to be the charm. "We had a decent time looking at the pictures," Randy said. "To tell you the truth, I was kinda sorry when Whisky had to leave to get x-rayed."

SEVENTEEN

Taking the metro to school with Pretty Boy had become a habit. He'd get on a few stops ahead of me and we'd meet up in the third metro car. If it wasn't too crowded, he'd save me a spot.

The morning after the open house, he wasn't on the metro.

I tried texting him, but he didn't answer, which was unusual for Pretty Boy.

No big deal, I told myself, right?

When I got close to New Directions, I noticed that Whisky wasn't smoking on the front porch. Maybe he was taking the day off on account of his nose. One thing was for sure: he wouldn't be in the boxing ring for a while. Hopefully, he'd still be able to do the warm-ups with Di.

It felt weird not seeing Pretty Boy or Whisky. Somewhere along the line, I'd gotten into a routine, gotten used to New Directions and the kids who went there. Maybe having to fight for the school's survival had made me feel more connected. I hoped that what had happened the night before hadn't made things too much worse.

Mom and I had discussed the situation on our drive home after the open house. She said she was impressed by the way Big Ron handled things. She liked his closing speech and what he'd said about none of us being perfect.

Then Mom did something she hardly ever does. She took her hand off the gearshift (she always keeps her hand on the gearshift), took my hand and squeezed it. Hard. The way she did when I was little. I didn't expect such a small gesture to feel so good.

"Why do you suppose he's so overweight?" Mom asked.

"Who?"

"Who else?"

"Oh, you mean Big Ron." I don't know when I stopped thinking of him as fat. He was just Big Ron. "How should I know?" I didn't mean to be rude—it just came out that way. Besides, what gave Mom the right to speculate about Big Ron's weight?

"I bet it's emotional eating," she said to the steering wheel.

"Since when are you a psychologist?"

Neither of us said anything more. But the spell that had started when Mom squeezed my hand was broken.

Florence came rushing out of her house when I walked by on my way to school. She must've been lurking behind the lace curtains, waiting to pounce. Her hands were planted on her hips.

"Hey you! Tessa!" she shouted as I passed her tiny front yard. "I've already been in to talk to your teacher and that boxing coach of yours. I guess they'll be filling you in soon. My house got robbed last night while I was at the open house! What do you think about that, hey?"

I couldn't blame her for being upset—getting robbed must be horrible—but it sounded like she was upset with *me*, as if she thought I'd had something to do with it.

"That's awful," I told her. "I'm really sorry. But that doesn't mean you have a right to be mad at me." I wasn't used to talking back to adults. (My mother didn't really count. Everyone talks back to their mother.) But I was glad I'd said it.

"So you don't think someone at that school of yours"— the way she said the word *school* suggested she didn't think there was much schooling going on at New Directions— "robbed me last night?"

"No, I don't think so."

It would have been more accurate to say, *I sure hope not*. Because if last night's fight was bad publicity for New Directions, a robbery at the house next door was probably worse.

"Well, I think you're wrong," Florence said. "And I'm going to prove it. If I do, you know what'll happen, don't you?"

I knew Florence wanted me to say that if she was right, the school board would be more likely to shut down New Directions. I turned my back and kept walking.

I didn't see the point of equations. Who would I ever discuss Pythagoras's theorem with? I was thinking all that when the police cruiser stopped in front of the house next door.

Randy rushed to the window, where he began giving us a full report—Randy-style. "Two…uh…cops just rang the doorbell. She's letting them in. The lady cop's got a notebook."

"Randall," Miss Lebrun said, "back to your seat, please. Now." Miss Lebrun's voice was calm, but I noticed she was tapping the desk. I'd never seen her do that before.

"Oh, c'mon, Miss Lebrun," Di said. "We're all dying to know what's going on over there. Admit it—even you are."

"I'll admit," Miss Lebrun said, and I could tell she was choosing her words carefully, "that I am curious. But if you're planning to pass the provincial math exam, you need to work on equations, not satisfy your curiosity. We all know the house next door was robbed last night. I just don't think it's the best idea for the police to spot any of you peering out the window right now."

Randy backed off when she said that.

If a right-angle triangle has a hypotenuse that measures 5 cm in length, and one of the sides has a length of 4 cm, then the length of the third side is—there was a loud, insistent rapping on the front door of the school. It had to be the police. Who else would knock like that?

Miss Lebrun was tapping again. "I'll handle this," she said.

"What about Big Ron?" I called out. "Should I go downstairs and get him?"

Miss Lebrun gave me a sharp look, but then she smiled. "You wouldn't be suggesting, would you, Tessa, that I can't handle this on my own."

When Miss Lebrun went to the door, the rest of us got up from our desks so that we could hear better. I wanted to get closer to the hallway, but Di was in the way. Was it my imagination or was her stomach getting the tiniest bit round?

"Good morning, officers," we heard Miss Lebrun say. "How can I help you this morning?"

I remembered the first day of school, when I'd thought she was the receptionist. I wondered if the cops thought so too.

"There was a robbery last night at the house next door." The male cop was speaking. "We wanted to have a word with one of your students—Percy Dewitt. Is he available to talk to us?"

"He's absent," Miss Lebrun said. "But if you give me your card, I'll ask him to contact you as soon as possible.

For the record, Percy is a lovely young man. Very talented, too." Miss Lebrun said this loudly, and I wondered if she knew we were listening and wanted us to hear. "As a matter of fact, all of my students here are lovely—and talented."

"We've heard about some of Percy's talents," the female cop said. From her tone, I didn't think she was talking about Pretty Boy's butterfly people.

Pretty Boy turned up at lunchtime. I'd never seen him stoned before. His eyes were bloodshot and glazed, and he was talking more slowly than Randy. Plus, he kept laughing at things that weren't funny.

Like when we told him Florence's house had been robbed. "You gotta be kidding," he said, cracking up. "Serves the nasty bitch right." Then he cracked up again.

Miss Lebrun called Pretty Boy to the classroom for a private talk. From the kitchen, we heard him shouting, "Why the fuck do they want to talk to me? Sure I've been in juvie, but I'm not doing that kind of stuff anymore, I swear!"

We couldn't make out what Miss Lebrun said after that, but whatever it was, it seemed to calm Pretty Boy down.

Being stoned didn't help Pretty Boy's boxing. His reflexes were slow, and the way he kept laughing got on all of our nerves. In the end, Big Ron told him to sit on the bench.

I was practicing my combinations on the leather bag. But every time I punched, I thought of what I'd heard Pretty Boy tell Miss Lebrun. *I'm not doing that kind of stuff anymore.* With Miss Lebrun, he'd been talking about B & E's. But hadn't he said something similar to me about using drugs?

EIGHTEEN

Di had given up smoking, but when Jasmine lit up at recess, Di sniffed at the air like she wanted to eat it.

Jasmine took the cigarette out of her mouth and offered it to Di.

Di pushed Jasmine's hand away. "No way," she said.

Just then Florence came outside. This time, she was carrying a red plastic dustpan. When she noticed the three of us, she scowled. Then she muttered loudly enough that we could hear, "Punks!"

Jasmine sprang up from the chair she was sitting on. "Who do you think you are calling us punks like that?" she shouted.

I tugged on Jasmine's arm. "She's not worth getting upset about," I whispered.

"Why don't you try taking a few deep breaths?" Di said to Jasmine.

Jasmine rolled her eyes. "What do you think this is? Goddamn Lamaze class?"

"I'm serious," Di said. "Haven't you heard Big Ron say it's important to breathe from your belly? He says most people are shallow breathers. Besides, Tessa's right. That woman isn't worth getting upset about."

"Well, if anyone knows bellies," Jasmine said, "it's Big Ron." She laughed at her own joke.

"Speaking of bellies...I've been meaning to tell you guys. I've decided to keep the baby," Di said softly.

"You sure that's a good idea?" Jasmine asked.

"I'm sure." Di stroked her belly. "Mostly."

Jasmine ran her hand over the buzzed side of her head. "I guess maybe we could do a breathing exercise. If we're keeping the baby..."

"We?" Di was smiling.

"We," Jasmine said, nodding. "You know what they say— it takes a village to raise a child. We're your village, Di."

So the three of us ended up doing this breathing exercise Big Ron had taught them the year before. Di called out instructions. "You gotta inhale really deeply...so you feel it here." She stroked her belly again. Sometimes I got the feeling she was just looking for excuses to stroke her belly. "Then you exhale just as slowly. Try not to think about anything but your breathing."

I was surprised by how quickly Jasmine got into the breathing exercise—especially considering the cracks she'd been making. She even closed her eyes. The deep breaths softened her face. Maybe she spent so much of her life fighting—and not just in the gym—it was hard for her to turn it off.

Di's eyes were closed now too.

I tried closing mine and focusing on my breath the way Di had explained. But I couldn't. Not with Florence shuffling around in the yard next door and the tinkling sounds of glass.

I opened one eye. Florence was on her patio, sweeping up the mess. The shards of glass in her dustpan glittered in the sunlight.

Di must've sensed the exercise wasn't working for me. "C'mon, Tessa," she whispered, "at least try."

So I tried harder. This time, I felt my body start to relax. Deep breath in, deep breath out. I observed my stomach rising and falling, and for a little while, it worked. All I thought about was my breathing.

From far away, I heard the sound of Florence trudging back up her stairs and opening the back door to her house. Then more tinkling as she emptied the dustpan into the garbage.

Deep slow breath in. Deep slow breath out.

There was something weirdly magical about the three of us—four, if you included Di's baby—breathing together like that.

I was the one who broke the spell.

"I just thought of something," I said. "If someone broke *into* the house next door, why was there glass *outside*?"

Jasmine rubbed her eyes as if I'd just awakened her from a deep sleep.

Di said, "Oh my god! Tessa's right!"

If I was right, whoever had smashed Florence's window had been *inside* her house. Jasmine pointed out that it could still have been Pretty Boy. "That boy could break into a bank vault," she said. "And he did take off during open house. I saw him go."

"And we all know he hates Florence," Di added.

"That doesn't prove anything," I said. "We all hate her."

Jasmine and Di couldn't argue with that.

"Maybe she did it herself—staged a robbery so she could pin it on one of us." I was talking quickly. "It'd help build her case that having a school like New Directions is bad for the neighborhood."

"You know what I think, Tessa?" Jasmine said. "I think you've been watching too many cop shows."

"I don't know," Di said. "I think maybe she's on to something."

"Okay, here's what I don't get," Jasmine said. "Why didn't the cops figure it out?"

"You saw how long they were in there with her this morning—maybe ten minutes," I said to Jasmine. "They weren't exactly scouring the lawn for clues."

Even Jasmine was coming around to my idea. "Maybe it's true," she said. "Maybe. So what are you gonna do about it?"

"Talk to Florence," I said.

"She's a psycho," Di said.

"I talked to her at the open house. She may not be the friendliest," I said, "but she's not that bad."

"If you've been in and out of as many foster homes as I have, let's just say you know a psycho when you meet one."

All Jasmine said was, "You're nuts, Tessa."

Miss Lebrun had made Pretty Boy phone the cops. They were going to come by New Directions later to talk to him. Miss Lebrun and Big Ron both wanted to be there. Pretty Boy had been moping around since the phone call.

When I went in to try to talk to him, he was carving his initials into his desk with a razor blade.

"You sure that's a good idea?" I asked him.

Pretty Boy kept carving. Then, without looking up, he said, "So you think I robbed that bitch next door?"

"No," I said. I hoped I sounded like I meant it.

"Once you've been in juvie, you get blamed for everything." Pretty Boy didn't say it like he felt sorry for himself—more like he was reading a fact from a history book.

"I'd say people need to get to know you before they judge you," I told him.

Pretty Boy stopped carving. "You'd say that, would you?"

"Yeah, I would. That's the way it worked for me. You're not what I expected."

"What are you saying exactly, Tessa? Come on." At least now Pretty Boy was grinning. Maybe I'd cheered him up. "Spit it out."

"What I'm saying is, you're a lot smarter and nicer than I would have expected."

Then Pretty Boy did something else I never would have expected. He blushed.

When Florence opened the door, she scowled at me. "What do you want now?" she barked.

"I just want to ask some questions—about what happened here last night."

She didn't invite me in, but she didn't slam the door on me either. "Why?" she asked.

"Because I don't want my best friend"—I'd never called Pretty Boy that before, but the words felt right—"getting blamed for something he didn't do."

Florence put her hands on her hips. "What if he did do it?"

I ignored her question. "I noticed you cleaning up glass from the patio before. If someone broke into your house, shouldn't most of the glass have been *inside*?"

Florence was wearing what looked like a cross between a nightgown and a dress. I wondered if she'd sewn it herself. When she rubbed her eyes, I noticed she looked older and more tired than usual. She probably wasn't sleeping well. "I don't know what you're talking about."

"Whoever broke your window must have been inside— not outside."

I could see that Florence's house had the same layout as New Directions. There was a long hallway leading to the kitchen. One end of a scratched-up old piano was sticking out of the living room and into the hallway. There was an empty cut-glass vase on top of the piano.

"Does Eddie play piano?" I asked.

"Leave him out of this!" Florence said. "None of this has anything to do with Eddie!"

I took a step back. I was beginning to think maybe Di was right about Florence being a psycho. "I was just asking if he plays piano."

"Yes, he plays. He's good too. But he won't practice. Why am I telling you all this?" Florence threw her arms up into the air. I wasn't sure whether it was because Eddie didn't practice piano or because she felt she had told me too much.

A kid who refused to practice piano. Whose mother must have had to scrimp to pay for piano lessons—and to send him to private school.

I tried to imagine what it would feel like to be Eddie. Pressured by a stressed-out, demanding mother. Probably the poorest kid at that fancy private school. Possibly picked on by the other kids who went there. Rebellious. Definitely.

In his worst moments, Eddie probably hated his mom as much as those of us at New Directions did.

"Maybe Eddie needs you to cut him some slack," I muttered. I didn't say what I was starting to think: maybe Eddie was so frustrated and tired of his mom's demands that he wrecked her sunflowers. And maybe even robbed his own house.

Florence's face contorted. She reminded me of a pot about to boil over. "Did you come over here to give me child-rearing advice? Is that why you're here?"

"That isn't why I came over." I tried to keep my voice level. "I came to talk to you about the broken glass."

Florence had her hand on the doorknob. "I heard what you had to say. Now get out of here and let me get back to my sewing."

NINETEEN

"Why me?" I asked Mr. Turner when he said he needed me to represent New Directions at the town hall meeting that night.

"Because Miss Lebrun tells me you're a good speaker—"

"I am?" I didn't think I was. How can someone who's naturally quiet be a good speaker? Maybe Miss Lebrun had said I'd done all right on my class presentation. Of course, the competition wasn't tough. Di had skipped school the day of her presentation, Randy had stopped so many times that his was fifteen minutes over the maximum, and Pretty Boy had dozed off—twice—during his.

"And because you're presentable," Mr. Turner added.

That explained it. "You mean you want me because I'm not pregnant and I don't wear a feather boa?"

Mr. Turner looked down at the floor. At least he didn't try to deny it. That made me want to help him out.

"I'm sorry I haven't given you more notice, Tessa. I got tied up, first with the open house, then with the police."

"Okay, fine. I'll do it. Do I have to prepare a talk?" I asked him.

"A prepared talk is a good idea. You could write something up on cue cards. Miss Lebrun told me she'd let you work on it during English class. I could look over your notes if you'd find that helpful," he said.

"I don't think so. But hey, thanks for the offer."

They should have called it a community center meeting since it took place at the community center, not the town hall. I didn't know if Montreal North even had a town hall.

The community center smelled of mothballs and boxed cookies. There were a couple of Ping-Pong tables and three old ladies knitting in rocking chairs. "Nice to see a member of the younger generation taking advantage of the facilities," one of them said when I passed her.

The meeting was held in a small auditorium. I sat between Mr. Turner and Miss Lebrun. Big Ron was on Miss Lebrun's other side. We all sat in metal folding chairs. Big Ron's chair was making distressed sounds. I hoped it would hold up for the meeting.

Florence was there too, sitting across the aisle with a few other neighbors. She was wearing a dress with yellow sunflowers on it. Had she worn it on purpose—to remind us of the flowers that were destroyed—or did she just have a thing for sunflowers?

Mr. Turner lifted his hand to greet her, but she didn't wave back.

Florence stood up and went to the front of the room to speak first. Not surprisingly, she got pretty emotional. "I organized this meeting tonight because I'm worried," she said. "Not only for myself, but for my son. And for all the other innocent children who live in this neighborhood."

I could see her pause to let that remark sink in.

"By now, you've probably all heard that my house was robbed two nights ago."

There was a worried murmur from the rest of the audience.

Mr. Turner raised his hand. It felt strange to see a principal do that. "I just want to say," he called out, "that the robbery is currently under investigation. There's no reason to point fingers at my students."

Florence had a sandpapery laugh. "No reason? I think there's plenty of reason. I suppose you think it's pure coincidence that the house that got robbed happens to be right next door to New Directions?"

Mr. Turner was more of a fighter than I expected. He looked Florence straight in the eye and said, "That's exactly what it is, madam. Pure coincidence."

Mr. Turner spoke next. His face was shiny with sweat. "The kids who come to New Directions need a chance. I'm not saying they're angels. They aren't. But they've already faced a lot of judgment from people around them"—he didn't look at Florence, but I knew he meant her and people like her—"and what they need is for people to have faith in them. To believe they are capable of change. Your support of a school like New Directions is a sign of your faith in the future—not just my students' futures, but all of our futures."

Miss Lebrun clapped. I thought other people might start clapping too, but they didn't.

A man in the audience—I hadn't seen him at the open house—raised his hand. "Faith in the future is one thing," he said. "But why the boxing?"

Big Ron heaved himself up from his chair. "If you don't mind," he said, looking over at Mr. Turner, "I'd like to answer that question."

Mr. Turner nodded. "Go ahead," he said. Then he explained to the audience that Big Ron was our boxing coach.

I didn't expect someone who liked talking as much as Big Ron did to be nervous, but the way he shifted his weight from one foot to the other made me think it was maybe easier for him to talk to teenagers than a room full of angry adults.

"Boxing is a way to channel aggression. It doesn't make people more aggressive—it calms them down."

Someone in the audience laughed. Someone else called out, "But you're teaching them how to fight! Don't tell me you're going to try to deny that!"

"You're right. I'm teaching these kids how to fight. But I'm teaching them something way more important—how to survive when they got nothing left. When they're huffing and puffing and they wanna give up. That's when it really counts in boxing, ladies and gents. And you know what else?" He looked at the audience as if he expected them to know what he was going to say, and I realized he'd stopped being nervous. "Life is one big boxing ring."

"That's the most ridiculous thing I've ever heard!" Florence shouted.

Someone else got up and stomped out of the room.

But a man sitting in the front row nodded his head.

Florence was standing up in front of her chair. "The kids"—and I was surprised she used the words *kids* and not *delinquents*—"who go to New Directions are dangerous, and you know what you're doing, Big Ron? You're training them to be even more dangerous!"

There was a flutter in the audience, but I couldn't tell whether people were agreeing or disagreeing with Florence.

Mr. Turner stepped closer to the microphone. "Let's all just settle down," he said, his voice reaching every corner of the room. "I want you to meet one of the students who attends New Directions. Ladies and gentlemen, this is Tessa McPhail."

"What color would you say her hair is?" I heard someone at the back of the room ask.

"Burgundy," I said into the microphone.

I'd meant to review my cue cards, but I'd been so caught up in the squabbling that I hadn't had time.

I had planned to start by telling them about the things I was learning at New Directions, beginning with Miss Lebrun's writing exercises and how they helped me clear my head first thing every morning. How it didn't feel right *not* to start my day with an entry in my journal. Then I was going to talk about the training I'd been doing with Big Ron. How I'd built up my endurance, and how seeing a fight didn't rattle me the way it used to.

But once I looked at the strained faces in front of me, a different beginning came to me.

"I think I know how you feel," I said. "You're anxious. You're afraid." My mouth felt dry, but I knew I had to go on—Mr. Turner and the others were counting on me. "I know because that's exactly how I felt when I got sent to New Directions. I was afraid of the kind of kids I'd meet. I knew they were kids who hadn't made it in the regular system"—I was careful not to use the word *expelled*—"and I was really afraid when I heard the school had a boxing program. I was afraid I'd get the"—I had to catch myself so I wouldn't swear—"afraid I'd get beaten up.

"But you know what? I had nowhere else to go. Things didn't...well...they didn't work out for me at my old high school. I'd done some tagging, and that didn't sit too well with my last principal. Or my mom."

Someone in the middle of the crowd squirmed. "Are you saying you defaced public property, young lady?"

I looked over at Mr. Turner. He hadn't warned me that people might call out during my speech. Mr. Turner blinked once—quickly. I hoped he was trying to tell me I was doing okay. That I should keep talking.

"Yes," I said in the direction of the person who had called out, "I defaced public property." I nearly added that I didn't do that anymore, but it wouldn't have been true, and I knew that if I was going to be a convincing speaker, I couldn't lie.

"When I first met the other students...Look, I'll be honest. I thought I was better than them. But I was wrong. Every single student who goes to New Directions has a story, and some of the stories...well...they'd break your heart. I'm not trying to make you feel sorry for any of us, I'm just trying to make you understand that we're good kids. Real kids. Kids who deserve your"—I knew it was important to find the right words—"your support. And your respect."

The room had grown quiet. "I have to talk to you about the boxing too. It isn't what you think. Boxing isn't about beating someone up—or getting beaten up. It's about knowing you don't have to be afraid to stand up when you see something wrong. And that's why I said yes when Mr. Turner asked me to talk to you tonight."

There was a smattering of applause, then some more. When I took my seat, my legs were shaking.

Florence returned to the microphone without looking over at me. "We got a little more information tonight. Thank you for that."

That couldn't have been easy for Florence to say. Still, why did she feel she could speak for the whole crowd? And why did the others let her?

She straightened the bottom of her sunflower dress. "I just want to remind you we've got nearly a hundred signatures on our petition asking that the school be moved to another location. That's a lot of signatures."

One man stood up. He was small, and his head was as bald as a golf ball. "About that petition," he said, his voice rising as he spoke. "I've decided to withdraw my name. I'm thinking maybe there might be some other folks here tonight who share my sentiment."

"I do," said a woman sitting at the back.

Florence's hands were back on her hips. "I don't think anyone should do anything rash. I think we all need to reflect on what's best for our community. On what we can do to make this a safe place for our kids. We don't want to just react to events."

I stood up again. This time, my legs didn't tremble. "Isn't that exactly what you've been doing, Florence? Reacting to events? Maybe even overreacting?"

"Tessa makes a valid point," the bald man said.

Which is when I had two thoughts. Maybe I wasn't such a terrible public speaker. And maybe there was hope for New Directions.

When I unlocked our front door later that evening, I heard Mom talking to someone in the kitchen. She must have just gotten home. I'd phoned to explain I'd been asked to speak at the town hall meeting. She said she would have liked to come to hear me, but the regional director of the bank was in Montreal and there was an important meeting she couldn't get out of. I'd told her not to worry. "If you were there, I might get even more nervous," I'd said.

Cyrus was sitting at my usual spot at the kitchen table. Of course, he had his camera and tripod with him. "What are you doing here?" I said. It wasn't the friendliest greeting, but I hadn't expected him to be there—and I didn't like someone sitting in my chair.

Mom answered for him. "He just dropped by to see you and we got to chatting." If that was true, why was Mom giving me the impression I'd caught her doing something wrong—like smoking or kissing someone else's husband? "How did your talk at the town hall go?" she added quickly. Too quickly.

I sat down in the chair next to her. "It went okay. So"—I tried to keep my voice casual—"what were you two chatting about?"

"You," Cyrus answered. "We were chatting about you."

He should've known that would tick me off.

"I was telling Cyrus I'm more than a little concerned about what's been going on at New Directions," Mom said. At least she didn't call it *that school*.

"Yeah," Cyrus added. "She told me about the robbery next door, and about how one of the students is pregnant."

"Did she tell you about the guy who was in juvie?"

Cyrus didn't even realize I was being sarcastic. "No," he said, shaking his head, "she didn't mention that." He cleared his throat and looked right at me. "You might not want my opinion, but I'm giving it to you because I love you and I think you need to hear it." I softened for a second when he used the word *love*. I knew it couldn't have been easy for Cyrus to say that in front of my mom. "I think your mom's right to be concerned. New Directions isn't the right place for you. You're changing—"

I could feel myself getting pumped up the way I did when I was about to hit the punching bag. Cyrus could have announced he loved me in front of the whole city and it wouldn't have calmed me down. "That's one thing you're right about, Cyrus. I am changing. I'm changing more than you know. And you know what else? Don't go talking to me like you're my father. *New Directions isn't the right place for you.*" My imitation came out sounding meaner than I meant it to, but I didn't care.

Mom tensed up when I said the word *father*. Maybe she felt bad because I'd never really had one. But hey, it wasn't her fault he'd had an aneurysm. She tried patting my hand. Only this time, it didn't help. "Cyrus means well, honey. I'm concerned about some of the other students at New Directions. Maybe they're not the best influence. And Cyrus told me there's at least one boy who's been behaving inappropriately around you. Cyrus thinks—"

"Behaving inappropriately around me?" I leaned across the table toward Cyrus. "Are you talking about Randy Randy?"

"Even just his nickname..." Mom said.

"For god's sake, Mom, it's a nickname! Randy Randy happens to be a decent guy. You were talking to his parents at the open house."

"I was?"

"If anyone's been behaving inappropriately, it's Cyrus. He's obsessed with Randy Randy. Jeez, Cyrus," I said, "I wish you'd stop being such an idiot."

Cyrus crossed his arms over his chest. "I don't think I'm being an idiot. I saw how close Randy Randy gets to you, and I could tell from your body language he was making you uncomfortable. That you didn't know how to deal with him."

"Since when did you get to be an expert on body language?" I was so angry, I could have spit at him. Then he could interpret the meaning of that particular bit of body language!

Mom tried patting my hand again, but this time, I pulled my hand away. "Tessa…" Mom paused, and I knew it was because she had something else to say but was weighing whether now was the right time to say it. "On my lunch hour today, I did some research into home-schooling. I think that with a little support, I could help you finish the school year at home. You wouldn't have to travel all the way to Montreal North…" Mom let her voice trail off.

"This isn't about traveling to Montreal North, Mom, and you know it. I want to finish my year at New Directions. You two might never understand this, but I'm starting to like it there. A lot."

It had been a long night, full of emotion, and I could feel tears welling in my eyes. But there was no way I was going to cry in front of them. So I grabbed my backpack from the floor and took off.

I could have slammed the door behind me, but I didn't want to do that either. I wanted Mom and Cyrus to know I could control myself—and my own life.

I heard Cyrus hurrying down the stairs behind me. "Wait up, Tessa!" he called.

I felt his hand on my shoulder. "I'm only trying to protect you." He said it in a soothing voice, like he was a sane person talking to someone who wasn't. "It's hard for me to see you hanging out with lowlifes at that school…"

I turned around to face him. "Lowlifes?" I swear I could feel the anger surging through my body like an electric charge. "How dare you judge my friends like that!"

And then I did something I probably shouldn't have. Only I couldn't stop myself. I was too angry.

I took a swing at Cyrus. A tight hook to the body that socked him right in the stomach. He was so busy trying to get his tripod out of my way, he forgot to protect himself. I felt the soft flesh of his belly give way under my knuckles.

I didn't feel bad when Cyrus whimpered. I also didn't wait for him to recover.

"We're through," I told him, though I guessed by then Cyrus had figured that out for himself.

My heart was pounding like a drum—even my eyeballs felt like they were vibrating in their sockets.

That punch had taken me by surprise as much as it had Cyrus. I hadn't known I had it in me. I also hadn't tried to stop it. I'd let my anger and frustration rule me.

Big Ron was always saying boxing wasn't about violence. But I'd used the skills he'd taught me to hurt someone, and in the moment I'd done it, it had felt good. Amazing, even. Could Cyrus be right? Was boxing making me more aggressive?

It was only when I got to the end of our block that the tears came.

TWENTY

A person in control of her own life should not be blubbering in the street like some kid in grade two. A person in control of her own life should know where she is heading. Or at least have a general sense.

But I had no idea.

My first impulse—after I blew my nose and wiped the tears off my cheeks—was to go to New Directions. But it was past ten, so that didn't make much sense. It did make me realize, though, that in some strange way, I felt at home at New Directions. Maybe it was because I'd started to care about the other kids who went there. Hadn't I just called them my friends? Maybe it was because I'd gotten to know their stories. I'd never felt that way before about a school. Not even when I was in elementary school, back before I'd ever broken a rule.

So I just wandered around our neighborhood, pulling myself together and trying not to think about how I'd lost control and punched Cyrus. I tried distracting myself by checking for new tags—there was nothing interesting. When I was on streets with lots of houses, I wondered about the people who lived in them. Maybe everyone had a story, not just the troubled teens who went to New Directions. Were there other girls like me—learning to stand up for themselves, sometimes tripping up along the way?

That reminded me of a framed picture in our living room. Mom took it the day I learned to walk. Maybe all these years later, I was still learning.

I didn't plan to go to the Villa-Maria metro station—I just ended up there. I also didn't plan to take the metro and get off at Chinatown. It just happened. I only knew I had to keep moving. Movement—even the gentle sway of the metro car—helped me think.

Once I got there, I realized I had no idea what I'd do if the restaurant was closed—or if Jasmine wasn't working. All I knew was if I could choose anyone to talk to right then, it would be her. So when I approached the dumpling house and saw all the lights were out and the front door was barred, I suddenly felt sadder and more tired than I had all day.

Some shops on St-Laurent Boulevard were still open. A calico cat blinked at me from behind a grocery store window. If Florence saw that cat, I thought, she'd be on the phone, lodging a complaint with the health inspector.

I scratched the window where the cat was and he blinked again.

A moment later, he took off, his patchwork tail swishing behind him like a giant feather.

Because I had nothing else to do and nowhere else to go, I walked into the grocery store. I reached into my pocket for change so I'd be able to buy something. An Asian man looked at me from behind the cash register.

"I like your cat," I told him.

"What cat?" he said.

Maybe he thought I was the health inspector.

I walked to the back of the shop where the refrigerator was. There was still no sign of the cat. I was reaching in for a water bottle when Jasmine came around the corner. She was carrying a wire shopping basket filled with fruits and vegetables. Part of me envied her independence. Part of me was sorry that she had to buy her own groceries. She looked tired.

"Hey," I said when I spotted her.

"Did they like your speech?" Jasmine asked. She didn't seem surprised to see me.

"I don't know for sure, but I think so. A couple of people said they wanted to take their names off the petition. What is that thing anyhow?" I pointed to a vegetable—or was it a fruit?—in her basket. It was shaped like a cucumber, only it was mint-green and had a bumpy skin.

"It's a Chinese delicacy," Jasmine said. "Bitter melon. I like it stir-fried with eggs for breakfast. My mom used to make it." She looked down at the floor, and I wondered if she was remembering her mom.

"Is it hard?" I asked her. She gave me a puzzled look and I realized she thought I was talking about the bitter melon. "No, no, not that," I said. "I mean...not having either of them anymore."

"Very," she said. "But I'm used to it now. A person gets used to things."

"I never knew my dad." It wasn't something I told a lot of people.

"Never?" Jasmine seemed surprised.

"Never. He died a few weeks before I was born. Brain aneurysm. My mom says he was a lovely guy."

"My dad used to sing me Chinese songs. He had a terrible voice." Jasmine looked at me like she was seeing me for the first time. "Sorry about your dad," she said.

"I guess I've gotten used to it. Like you said. So, you heading home?" I asked.

"Home?" she said with a hard laugh. "Nah, I'm killing time."

"And buying groceries."

"Yeah," she said, "and buying groceries. Otherwise, there won't be anything to eat. What about you, Tessa Something-or-Other? What are you doing out so late?"

I put up my fighting guard when she called me that.

Jasmine laughed.

"I'm killing time too. Mom trouble." I felt bad after saying that. Jasmine probably wished she had a mom—even one who got on her nerves the way mine sometimes did. "And boyfriend trouble. You might find this hard to believe, but I just punched my boyfriend."

"Did he deserve it?" Jasmine asked.

"I guess. It felt good at the time. But afterward, I bawled like a baby."

Jasmine nodded. "That happens. It happened to me the first time I went into the ring. You get an adrenaline surge when you're fighting, then when it's over, you bawl your head off. It's perfectly normal, healthy even...How's your boyfriend?"

"I didn't stick around to find out. I should probably phone him later."

"Ever had a bubble tea?" Jasmine asked me when she was paying for her groceries.

"Bubble tea?"

"I guess that means no." Jasmine grabbed my hand. Then she pointed to a tea shop across the street. It was so small you could have walked by it a thousand times without noticing it. "My treat," she said.

Someone who didn't know us might have thought we were two ordinary teenage girls without a care in the world.

"Those bubble teas look like slushies," I told Jasmine when we squeezed into the tea shop and spotted an old couple sipping bubble tea through straws.

Jasmine snorted. "Do not compare bubble tea with a slushie. A slushie is a North American abomination. Bubble tea is an Asian delicacy."

"What *isn't* an Asian delicacy around here?" I asked.

Jasmine ordered two bubble teas from the girl behind the counter. They really did look like slushies, but I didn't want to risk offending Jasmine by saying so again.

"Bubble tea was invented in Taiwan," she told me.

It was so sweet it made my teeth tingle—and not in a good way. Then, when I took another sip—I knew if I didn't, Jasmine would take it personally—I nearly choked on something rubbery. I spit it back into the glass.

Jasmine laughed. "I should have warned you," she said. "It's got tapioca pearls in it."

The tapioca pearls took some getting used to. Still, it was nice to be sitting with Jasmine on two tall stools in the window of the tea shop. "So," she said, tapping her fingers on the counter. "I thought you were gonna dump your boyfriend a while ago."

"I was. It's just taking longer than I expected."

"You afraid to be alone? Is that it?" Jasmine asked.

"Maybe."

"We're all alone," she said, taking a long sip of bubble tea. "Each and every one of us."

"Who knew you were such a philosopher?"

"Must be Big Ron rubbing off on me."

We laughed so hard, we nearly choked on our tapioca pearls.

Jasmine groaned when her cell phone rang. "It'll be my aunt. Telling me she won't be home until tomorrow morning. And that we're out of milk. Or juice. Or eggs."

She let the phone ring a few more times before she took it out of her purse.

But when she looked at the display, she said, "It's not my aunt. It's Di."

She smiled when she took the call. "Hey, Di," she said. "Isn't it way past your bedti—?" Jasmine's face froze.

I could hear Di sobbing on the other end of the line.

"Okay, stay calm." I got the feeling Jasmine was saying it as much to herself as to Di. "I've been doing some reading. Some bleeding is normal. It's called *spotting*. We'll be right there."

TWENTY-ONE

Jasmine flagged down the first cab that came by. "Royal Victoria Hospital," she told the driver as we piled into the backseat. "Now!"

"Yes, ma'am."

The driver didn't stop for the yellow light on René Lévesque Boulevard.

"Is she already at the hospital?" I asked Jasmine.

"She was on her way to the emergency room."

"So you've been reading up on…spotting," I said. The cab was going so fast, St-Laurent Boulevard was just a blur of lights.

"I found a used copy of *What to Expect When You're Expecting* at a garage sale." Jasmine made it sound as if she wouldn't have bought it otherwise.

"I thought you thought she should have an abortion." I whispered it, in case the driver was listening.

Jasmine gave me a sharp look. "What I thought doesn't matter much, does it?"

"Okay, okay."

The driver left us at the emergency-room entrance. An old man wearing a wrinkled hospital gown and hooked up to a portable IV drip was standing outside, smoking. I thought about Whisky and his dad, both addicted to cigarettes.

I followed Jasmine to the reception desk. Every face we passed was strained and tense. I knew my face looked like that too.

A Plexiglas wall separated us from the receptionist. She was filling in a chart. Jasmine spoke to her through a round opening in the Plexiglas. "We're here to see our friend Diane Braithwaite."

"She's already inside." The receptionist pointed to a gleaming metal door at the end of the hallway. Her face didn't give anything away.

"Is the baby okay?" I asked.

"I'm afraid I can't give you any information." The receptionist looked at me and then at Jasmine. "Only one of you can go in at a time," she said. Then she picked up her pencil and went back to her chart.

"You go," I told Jasmine when we reached the metal door. Even from outside, we could hear machines pinging. "You two are best friends."

The silver door flew open as a nurse exited.

"Out of the way, please," someone else said. Two cops were helping an orderly wheel a gurney into the emergency room. Someone was strapped onto the gurney. I saw blood. My stomach lurched, and I turned away.

Jasmine grimaced. Before the door could close behind the gurney, she looked over her shoulder both ways, then tugged on my hand and dragged me inside with her. There wasn't time to object or point out that we were breaking hospital rules.

We heard Di's sobs before we saw her. I looked down the hallway and spotted the toes of a pair of silver cowboy boots sticking out from behind a long green curtain. "She's in there," I told Jasmine.

We rushed over and pulled open the curtain. Di was lying on a gurney, wearing a hospital gown; her legs were covered with a white hospital sheet. Her face was almost as white as that sheet. Her whole body was shaking.

Big Ron was there too. He was resting one of his giant paws on her shoulder. "Everything is gonna be okay, Lady Di," he kept saying. He looked worried though.

Jasmine wanted to hug Di, but Big Ron stopped her. "Better not do that," he whispered. "She's still a little tender down there."

"Okay, I found you some water." Randy poked his head in from behind the curtain and held out a paper cup with water in it. Pretty Boy was behind him.

Randy handed Di the water. She took a tiny sip.

Randy came to stand next to me. I could feel the heat from his body.

"Is the baby okay?" Jasmine's voice broke. She pushed her hair out of her face, wiping her eyes with the back of her hand. Later, I wondered if she'd been crying.

Di shook her head and sobbed some more.

A nurse and a doctor came into the curtained-off cubicle. "Some of you are going to have to wait in the waiting room," the nurse said, but at least she didn't sound annoyed.

Jasmine stayed with Di. The rest of us filed out of the cubicle. But we didn't go to the waiting room the way the nurse had told us to. We just stood outside the cubicle in a sad, quiet clump. The nurse was too busy to notice.

"Can you tell us what happened, Diane?" we heard the doctor ask.

Di's words were punctuated by sobs. Randy and Pretty Boy both took a few steps down the hallway. I knew they wanted to give Di some privacy.

"It started with these terrible cramps," Di said.

"Abdominal cramps?" the doctor asked.

"Yeah, and in my lower back too. Like when I get my period, only worse. Then I noticed the spotting." Di sniffled. "So I came straight to the hospital. It's what they told us to do at prenatal class."

Di hadn't told me she'd been going to prenatal class. My heart was breaking for her. Even before her baby was born, she was trying to be a good mother. I knew it was because she wanted to be a better parent than her own parents had been.

"Did anything happen after that?" It was the nurse talking now. Her voice was gentle, but I could feel her digging for information.

"The cramps got so bad I could hardly move." Di's voice had turned eerily calm. "I swear, I thought I was going to die. I went to the bathroom. Just outside the emergency room. I…I never saw so much blood. It was everywhere. I made a terrible mess. And I think I saw—" And now Di exploded into tears. She cried so hard, the green curtain shook.

Neither the doctor nor the nurse asked Di what she thought she had seen. I didn't want to imagine it.

"These things happen, unfortunately," the doctor said. "I'm going to need to examine you. Are you okay with that, Diane?"

Di whimpered during the examination.

The doctor whispered some instructions to the nurse. I leaned in to listen, but I couldn't hear what he was saying.

Ten minutes later, the doctor emerged from the cubicle, his face grim. That's when I knew for sure Di had lost her baby.

Miss Lebrun showed up about fifteen minutes later, carrying her bicycle helmet. Her face was flushed and she was out of breath.

"Sorry it took me so long," she told Big Ron. "I had trouble finding a babysitter."

Miss Lebrun had a baby? How could she not have told us that?

"I'm going to go in and see her," Miss Lebrun said.

I nudged Big Ron. "I didn't know she had a baby."

"He's not exactly a baby anymore. The kid's almost seven."

Big Ron must've seen me trying to do the math in my head. If Miss Lebrun was twenty-three, maybe twenty-four tops, she couldn't have been any older than...

"She was seventeen when she had him," Big Ron said.

The same age as Di.

No wonder Miss Lebrun had been looking out for her.

Di was going to need some surgery that was standard procedure after a miscarriage. The surgery was scheduled for the next morning, and if everything went well, she'd be released from hospital that afternoon. Miss Lebrun wanted to stay overnight at the hospital, so we sat with Di while Miss Lebrun called her babysitter.

Di tried to sit up a little on the gurney. "What about Ruger?" she managed to ask.

"Won't the people at your house look after him?" I could tell Miss Lebrun was trying not to say *foster parents*.

Di bit her lip. "They won't be happy about it. They only let me bring Ruger with me on condition that I'd be the one looking after him."

"Don't worry about Ruger. Someone's already offered to look after him," Big Ron said.

Di slumped back onto the gurney. "Who?" she asked.

Big Ron grinned. "Mr. Turner. Turns out he's got a thing for pit bulls. He and his wife are thinking of getting one of their own."

Because there was so little room in Di's cubicle, we took turns going in to tell her we were sorry.

Pretty Boy was first. "Look," I heard him tell Di, "maybe it's better this way. Maybe there was something wrong with the—"

Di cut him off with her sobbing. But it was Jasmine who sent Pretty Boy packing. "Would you take your sweet ass out of here this instant?" she said. "That's the very last thing Di needs to hear right now."

"Okay, okay, I'm really sorry." Pretty Boy sounded almost as nervous as he had the night his brothers were hassling him. "But there's just one more thing—"

"Well say it then!" Jasmine barked.

Pretty Boy lowered his voice, but we could all still hear him. "I just want to say I love you, Di. We all do. That's why we're here."

I hadn't cried when I heard Di had lost her baby. But now—when Pretty Boy said that—I couldn't seem to stop.

Because there weren't any rooms available, Di had to sleep in the cubicle. We helped make Miss Lebrun a nest from two vinyl chairs and as many blankets as we could find. "Don't worry about me," she said as she swept us out of the cubicle. "I'll be fine."

We were too wired to go home, so we all said yes when Big Ron suggested we have a cup of tea in the hospital cafeteria. But because it was late, the cafeteria was closed.

We settled for vending-machine tea. Big Ron insisted on treating us. He emptied six whole sugar bags into his Styrofoam cup. If he ever went on a diet, he could start by using Sweet'N Low.

Jasmine bit her lip. "What if Di gets really depressed? Some women have a hormone surge after a miscarriage."

"Since when," Big Ron asked, raising his eyebrows, "do you know so much about pregnancies and miscarriages?"

"She's been reading up," I told him.

Big Ron slurped his tea. "If she does get depressed—and it may not happen," he said, "you guys'll be there for her. Just like you were here for her tonight."

"Did you know Miss Lebrun had a kid?" I asked Jasmine and Pretty Boy.

"Why's it such a big deal to you?" Jasmine asked instead of answering my question. I decided that meant she knew. Pretty Boy said he hadn't.

I tried to find the right words. "It's just that...I guess I thought I knew her."

Big Ron rubbed his hands on his thighs. "People are entitled to some privacy," he said.

Pretty Boy twirled one end of his electric-blue feather boa. "Does that mean you're keeping secrets from us too, Big Ron?"

Big Ron took another slurp of tea. "I got no comment," he said. Then he looked at his watch. "I nearly forgot to tell you guys something. Since Miss Lebrun is gonna be late for school tomorrow, you'll be spending the whole day in the gym with me. And Tessa Something-or-Other,"—he looked over at me—"I think you're about ready for a little sparring. Jabbin' Jasmine, you're gonna have to promise to be gentle."

TWENTY-TWO

I shut the bathroom door so Mom wouldn't see what I was doing: practicing my moves in front of the mirror.

Protect yourself! Big Ron's voice boomed in my head. I brought my wrists closer to my cheeks. *Rotate your hips! Put some power in those punches!* he boomed again. I rotated my hips.

"That's better!" That was me, talking to my reflection.

Mom and I ate our granola together. When I'd come in the night before, she was waiting up. I'd told her about my argument with Cyrus and about Di's miscarriage. Mom was shocked that I'd punched Cyrus and glad when I told her I planned to phone him to apologize. Then she apologized for upsetting me. All she wanted, she kept saying, was the best for me, and would I just consider the homeschooling option? I'd told her I wouldn't. That I didn't want to talk about it anymore.

So I decided it was better not to mention that I'd be sparring today. It would only set her off on another worry binge.

Except it's hard to keep a secret from my mom. She added milk to her cereal. "You're jumpy," she said.

"I'm fine. Just fine."

"If you were fine, you wouldn't say so twice. Maybe you're still processing everything that happened last night—with Cyrus and then at the hospital. It sounds like you and your friends went through a lot."

I brought a spoonful of granola to my mouth. "Does this count as emotional eating?" I asked her.

"Tessa McPhail, are you mocking me?" Mom did not sound amused.

I swallowed the granola. "Maybe…" I said to my empty spoon.

"Look at me," Mom said.

I put down my spoon and looked at her.

"I'm trying to be supportive," she said. "You don't always make it easy for me."

"I know," I said sheepishly. "You're right. Sometimes a person just needs to figure stuff out for herself."

Big Ron handed me a crumpled plastic bag. Inside were my new red polyethylene boxing gloves. They didn't smell as delicious as leather ones, but they were a great shade of red and no one's sweaty hands had ever been inside them. There were also some breast protectors and a plastic mouthpiece in the box. "No hurry to pay me back for those," he said. "Your credit's good with me."

I examined the breast protectors. They were plastic inserts in a bra that looked like it was designed for a dominatrix. "A woman doesn't want to get hit there," Big Ron said. I knew he was making a point of *not* looking at my chest. "Not any more than a guy wants to get hit where the sun don't shine."

That morning we spent the first hour in the gym warming up, doing cardio, then stretching out our legs. Every time my eyes landed on the boxing ring, I felt a flutter in my stomach, as if a bird had landed there.

I went into the bathroom to put on the breast protectors. Let's just say I wouldn't be auditioning for the Victoria's Secret catalog anytime soon.

Jasmine was already in the ring, shadowboxing.

My heart thumped double-time underneath the molded plastic. "You trying to spook me or what?" I figured if I made a crack, she wouldn't guess how nervous I was.

"Who, me?" She danced over and jabbed me with her elbow. "I promised Big Ron I'd be gentle," she said. "But he doesn't call me Jabbin' Jasmine for nothing!"

The bird in my belly fluttered again when I squeezed between the ropes and into the ring.

I shadowboxed in my corner, but I felt like a fake. Jasmine had rhythm. I was a frightened robot.

I knew I had to loosen up. But thinking that only made me more robotic.

Pretty Boy, Whisky and Randy were watching from the bench. I wished Di was there too.

Big Ron cleared his throat. Speech time. "At the sound of the bell," he said, "you're going to box the first of three two-minute rounds. Remember, you have to follow my instructions at all times. When I tell you to stop or break, you stop punching. You take a couple of steps back and you don't re-engage until I say 'Box!' again. Jabbin' Jasmine, remember to put a little water in your wine. I want you to treat Tessa Something-or-Other like a fighter, but I don't want you going too hard either. You got that, ladies?"

Jasmine bobbed her head. "Got it!"

I just nodded. I was already too winded to speak—and we hadn't even started sparring.

The bell sounded. I kept my guard up. When I saw Jasmine's left hook coming at me, I gulped, but at least I didn't freeze. I wove to my left, just avoiding contact.

"Nice weave!" Randy called out. His voice seemed far away.

I felt the blood rush to my head as I moved out of Jasmine's range. I might've been moving like a robot, but she hadn't hit me yet.

I could feel Big Ron's eyes boring into us, watching every move, anticipating what would happen next. He must've known I was terrified. Maybe he'd seen my thighs shaking. "It's good to be afraid, Tessa Something-or-Other," he called from the ropes. "Fear can freeze you. Fear can grab hold of you. But fear can also keep you safe. If you don't have any fear, you're vulnerable."

Well then, I wasn't vulnerable.

I moved in on Jasmine. For a split second, our eyes met. I half expected her to wink. But she didn't. I didn't see anything in her eyes—not recognition, not laughter. Just focus. That was what made her such a fine boxer.

I threw a straight punch, aiming for her cheek. Jasmine dove out of the way. But she came back at me. I wove to the left, not quickly enough this time. She hit me in the gut, where the bird was. It hurt. I dropped one hand to my belly.

"Keep your guard up!" Big Ron hissed.

I brought my hand back up to my face just in time. Jasmine was coming at me again. Every part of me dripped sweat. Even parts I didn't know could get sweaty—like the insides of my elbows.

The round must be almost over.

"A minute and a half left!" Big Ron called out.

A minute and a half? There had to be something wrong with the timer! But I didn't say those things. I screamed them inside my head. I was too busy ducking and weaving.

I stepped back to the ropes, keeping low. I needed to catch my breath, regroup. The ropes quivered against my back.

"You're doing great!" Pretty Boy shouted. Did he mean me or Jasmine?

She came after me, both gloves in front of her face. Rather than backing away, I moved in on her. She dropped her elbow. I reached for her elbow, then wrapped both my arms around the back of her arm, tying her up. Neither of us could move.

"No holding! Break!" Big Ron shouted. I tried to slow my breathing and catch my breath. But I couldn't. My breath was a horse galloping away from me.

When would the round be over? I'd been training so hard for so many weeks. Why wasn't I tougher?

"All right, it's time to box again!" Big Ron bellowed.

I sent my fists flying, one after the other. I could hear Jasmine snorting as she ducked and wove. Was she laughing at me, or was it possible Jasmine was getting tired too?

The bell sounded. I had thought the round would never end, but it did.

Randy brought me water and clapped my shoulder. I was too tired to thank him. But not too tired to feel a little spark when his fingers touched my skin. I let the water sit in my mouth before it trickled down my throat.

"You ladies nearly ready for round two?" Big Ron wanted to know.

I ran my tongue over the plastic mouthguard. I wasn't capable of forming words, but I could grunt. So I grunted yeah. I was ready. At least, I hoped I was.

The second round was worse. I stumbled, not bobbing and weaving as quickly as I had before. Every move was a colossal effort. I tried to keep my breaths quick and short.

"Mix it up! Work your combinations!" Big Ron called from outside the ropes.

Jasmine landed three punches in that round. Two more to my belly. One to my jaw. I could feel my lower lip swelling up.

"You ladies ready for the third and final round?" Big Ron asked.

I remembered what Big Ron had taught us. *What counts most is what you do when you've got nothing left.* I had nothing left.

This time all I could do was nod.

"You're doing great!"

I knew Randy meant me. But I knew I wasn't doing great. Not even close. My legs were collapsing underneath me. I had nothing left. Nothing at all. I couldn't even extend my arm for a straight punch. I was flailing. My arms had turned to pulp.

Jasmine threw another punch. I couldn't duck anymore. I didn't have the energy. She got me in the belly again—this time with a straight punch. Even keeping up my guard took more than I had. I felt my upper arms lose strength, my hands drop from my face. *Keep up your guard! Protect yourself!*

I couldn't tell anymore if it was Big Ron talking or me hearing his voice inside my head.

What counts most is what you do when you've got nothing left.

I forced my hands back up to my face. I thought about the hockey riot. I'd been a little girl, unable to protect myself or my mom. I'd just taken it. Let myself get trampled. Two years later, when those bullies had tormented Rachel, I'd run away when she most needed my help. If I'd stood up to those girls, things might have turned out differently. But I'd been too afraid.

I couldn't feel like that again. Not even here in a boxing ring.

Maybe remembering all that gave me a second wind.

I breathed in. Jasmine wasn't dancing so quickly anymore. And she'd dropped her guard from her left cheek. When she turned toward me, I saw my opportunity. I came back with a left hook. It landed *bam!* underneath her jaw. She winced. I punched again. My punches were coming from all angles.

Jasmine rallied, driving a straight right-hand punch to my rib cage. But I was beyond feeling pain.

I ducked, narrowly missing Jasmine's left hook.

The bell sounded and I slumped forward like a rag doll. I still couldn't talk. I was too zonked even to sigh.

"Good work in there, ladies!" Big Ron shouted, his voice sounding hoarse. Then he turned to the boys on the bench. "I don't know about the rest of you, but I'd say Tessa earned herself a new nickname today. Something-or-Other doesn't do her justice anymore. You gentlemen got any suggestions?"

"The octopus!" It was Pretty Boy's idea. "The blue-ringed octopus!"

"I get the octopus part. Tessa flails her arms around like an octopus. But what's with the blue rings?" Whisky asked.

"The blue-ringed octopus is the only one that presents a danger to humans. And from what I saw today, Tessa Blue-Rings is one dangerous mollusk."

"I like the sound of Tessa Blue-Rings," Whisky said. "Tessa the Blue-Ringed-Octopus is too long."

I was too exhausted to object.

TWENTY-THREE

I'd never felt mellower as I walked from New Directions to the metro.

All the fight was out of me. It was a shame I hadn't been in the ring before the town hall meeting. If I had, I would have tried to describe the feeling.

I was noticing things I'd never noticed before—how bugs had feasted on a ropy vine, turning the leaves to green lace; the way the sun made a telephone wire glisten; the sharp smell of coffee drifting up from someone's basement apartment. How could I have walked along the same street so many times without noticing any of this?

I was tired and sore, but it was a delicious tired and sore. When I got home, I'd soak in the tub. Maybe use the arnica oil Mom had bought at the health-food store when

I'd started boxing. She'd read somewhere that it was good for sore muscles.

I tested the thought of Mom in my mind. I remembered how adamant she'd been about homeschooling me. But I didn't feel angry anymore. What Mom had said was true. She did want the best for me. Only she didn't know what the best was. I couldn't blame her for that.

Because thinking of Mom wasn't upsetting me, I tried something harder—Cyrus. Was I so mellow from sparring that thinking about him wouldn't upset me? I was treading on thin ice. I'd have to go carefully if I didn't want to sink down into my angry feelings.

I pictured Cyrus on that rooftop in Chinatown, droning on about his dreams. He was entitled to his dreams. We all were. Who knew—maybe Cyrus would find a way to make his come true. Maybe making a career in photography would be more like boxing than Cyrus realized. Maybe even if Cyrus was the most focused person in the world, there'd come a time when he had nothing left and, if he really *really* wanted to make it, he'd have to keep going anyway. Maybe I could tell him that.

Then I remembered coming home and finding Cyrus in the kitchen with Mom. How puffed up he had been with certainty that he knew best—and how jealous and possessive he'd acted. Remembering the scene still bothered me, but it didn't enrage me the way it had when it happened.

Of course, I also remembered punching Cyrus in the stomach. The way his flesh had given way underneath my knuckles, the shocked look on his face.

Hitting Cyrus was a mistake. I owed him an apology.

I tried his cell, but it went right to voice mail and I didn't think I should apologize in a message. That would have been too easy.

I'd built up a lot of heat in the boxing ring, but now I felt a sudden chill. When I looked up at the sky, I noticed the sun had disappeared behind a ridge of clouds. I'd learned from Cyrus to notice when the sky was beautiful—and right then, it was. As soon as that thought registered, another one occurred to me. Cyrus might have been avoiding my call. But I also knew where Cyrus had to be—back on the rooftop in Chinatown.

When I got out of the metro, I could see a figure on the roof. Cyrus.

Mr. Lee's eyes widened when he saw me. "What in god's name happened to you?" he asked. "Cyrus didn't do that to your lip, did he?"

I looked him straight in the eye. "Of course not. I'm a boxer." It was the first time I'd ever said that about myself. "I need to go talk to him. I won't be long."

"Go ahead then," Mr. Lee said. "I'm not going to argue with a boxer."

When I got up to the roof, I was surprised to find Cyrus looking out at Chinatown. "I thought you didn't like that view," I said.

Cyrus jumped when he heard my voice.

"What are you doing here?" he asked without turning around to face me.

"I came to apologize. I shouldn't have hit you. I'm really sorry."

"I was more surprised than anything else," Cyrus said. "You didn't punch me that hard."

"You didn't protect yourself. It's one of the first things you learn when you box."

Cyrus finally turned around. "Oh my god!" he said. "What happened to your mouth?"

I told Cyrus how I'd sparred for the first time. That I'd done okay. That I kept going even when I thought I had nothing left. I started telling him it might be like that for him in the photography world too. "Your photos could get rejected by an agency or a gallery…you'd be crushed, you might want to give up…but you'd have to keep going. If it really mattered, you'd have to…"

Cyrus wasn't listening. He touched my swollen cheek, and I winced. He bit his lip. I wouldn't have minded so much if he acted sympathetic, not that I needed anyone's sympathy.

What I didn't want was a lecture.

Or for Cyrus to get angry.

What I got was an angry lecture.

"You can't keep boxing! I won't let you!" Cyrus yelled. The only good thing about arguing on a rooftop is that nobody can hear you. But then I remembered Mr. Lee—was he watching us on his closed-circuit TV monitor?

"You won't *let* me? Do you *hear* yourself, Cyrus?"

That last question hung in the air, a kite drifting in the moody sky around us.

Cyrus dropped his hands to his sides.

"I don't need your permission to do anything." I spat out the words—where was my mellow now? "Do you understand, Cyrus? I'm in charge of my own life. Look, I'm sorry I punched you last night. Really I am. I lost control and that was wrong. But it's over, Cyrus. We're over."

I saw one small tear in the corner of Cyrus's eye. I thought about wiping it away, but I didn't.

"I just don't want you getting hurt," he whispered. "You can't blame me for that."

"I'm not afraid of getting hurt. Not anymore. I'm afraid of *not living.*"

Cyrus didn't say anything to that. Maybe, for once, I'd actually gotten through to him. Because I wasn't sure when I'd be speaking to him again, I decided there was one more thing I needed to tell him.

"You're an amazing photographer, Cyrus. You see stuff other people miss. Remember those balloons? It's your openness to things that makes your photos magic. But you know something? It works with people too. Being open—instead of judging them."

Cyrus looked across the street at the other gray stone building. I knew he was imagining the photos he'd shoot. "I shouldn't have judged you," he whispered.

"Or my friends," I added.

I didn't notice my mom's gray sedan parked across from the Villa-Maria metro. It was only when I heard honking that I realized she was there waiting for me. My first thought was Cyrus must've phoned her to say I'd gotten whacked in the face. It would be just like him to keep interfering in my life even after we'd broken up. Had I ever actually liked that about him? If I had, it was because I'd been a different Tessa. Tessa Something-or-Other. Not Tessa Blue-Rings.

If Mom noticed my lip and cheek, she didn't say anything. Which must've been hard for her. She also didn't mention Cyrus. Maybe he hadn't called her.

"Why're you here?" I asked as I buckled my seat belt.

Mom was already making an illegal U-turn. Which meant this was an emergency. "Because we're going to the casino."

"The casino? Mom, have you lost your mind?"

Mom kept her eyes on the road. "Jasmine tried phoning you. She figured you were on the metro. So she phoned the apartment. Told me all the money she's been saving from her job was stolen. She's pretty sure her aunt took it.

She says the aunt gambles. I said I'd get you and we'd meet her at the casino."

"You told her what?"

When Mom got on the Ville-Marie Expressway, she was gunning it so hard that no one honked or tried passing her. It was the first time I'd driven with my mom on a highway and she didn't swear. Not once.

Jasmine was at the entrance to the casino, waiting for us. She was wearing bright-red lipstick and the long half of her hair was tied back in a sleek ponytail.

Mom eyed the guard at the wicket. "I just realized," she said, "that you have to be eighteen to get in. I may have to go in alone. Do you have a picture of your aunt, Jasmine, so I can recognize her?" Mom was using her assistant-manager voice.

"That's my aunt Melinda." Jasmine lifted her chin to a wall of black-and-white headshots outside the wicket. Jasmine's aunt was younger than I'd expected. She had Jasmine's dark hair and eyes, but her face was more angular.

"What's her picture doing—?" I stopped myself when I noticed the information above the photos. *These individuals have requested not to be allowed into the casino.* I did a quick calculation—there were at least two hundred photos on the wall. But if Jasmine was right, her aunt Melinda had gone into the casino anyhow.

"Don't worry about us getting in," Jasmine said, pulling a fake ID card out of her wallet. I recognized the Concordia University logo.

Mom gave me a sharp look. "You have one of those too?"

"Mine's McGill."

Mom sighed. "I did my best to raise you right. Honest I did. How long have you had that thing?"

There didn't seem to be any point in lying. "Since grade eight."

"Grade eight?"

"Every kid's got fake ID, Mom."

"Not Cyrus."

It was my turn to give Mom a sharp look. "Even Cyrus."

The guard glanced at our ID cards and nodded. "Have you got ID?" he asked my mom. She giggled. Were they flirting? Gross!

I'd been to the Casino de Montréal before, so I knew what to expect. A maze of slot machines on the ground floor. People—mostly seniors—cranking up the machines. Lots of clanging—one old woman scooping up a mountain of coins. Other people circling her, hoping to catch some of her luck.

The light was bright, almost glaring, but there were no windows. "The people who run this place don't want visitors knowing what time it is. Whether it's even day or night," Mom explained as we followed Jasmine up the gleaming escalator to the third floor, where the blackjack tables were.

"The high-stakes tables are over there," Jasmine said, pointing straight ahead.

"How much did she take?" I asked her.

"Twenty-three hundred." She sounded more tired than angry. I got the feeling this wasn't the first time Aunt Melinda had found Jasmine's stash.

I sucked in my breath. That was a lot of nights cleaning floors at the dumpling shop.

"I was too busy between school and work to take it to the bank. So I was keeping it in my mom's Bible. Can you believe she looked in there?"

I couldn't tell if I was supposed to answer.

Mom reached for Jasmine's hand and squeezed it. "The main thing is we're here, and we're going to find your aunt Melinda and bring her home and get her some help."

It sounded like a tall order.

Jasmine was as focused now as she'd been in the boxing ring. She slipped by half a dozen tables, scanning the faces of the people gathered at each one. Most were sitting on stools. Others were standing behind them.

"Good evening, ladies. Care to join us?" a dealer called to us. He was wearing a tuxedo shirt and black bow tie. Jasmine glided past him without answering.

"See that guy's fat ass?" Jasmine asked me, lifting her eyes in the direction of a gambler leaning over a blackjack table.

She was right. He had a huge ass. Maybe gamblers needed more exercise.

"He's wearing a diaper."

"Tell me you're kidding."

"I'm not kidding. Lots of them do. That way they don't have to get up to use the can."

I tried not to inhale.

"That's my aunt Melinda." Why was Jasmine pointing to a blond woman wearing a tight dress with black sequins? She didn't look too Asian to me.

Mom must've been thinking the same thing. "Are you absolutely sure, dear?" she asked Jasmine.

Aunt Melinda must have disguised herself to get into the casino. I couldn't imagine being so desperate to lose money—though, of course, Aunt Melinda was hoping to *win* money, not lose it. Judging by the anxious faces I'd seen so far in the casino, more people were losing than winning.

"Aunt Melinda!" Jasmine started marching to the table, but Mom put a hand on her shoulder and stopped her.

"Let me talk to her," Mom said.

I had to hold Jasmine back. A security guard was watching us from the corner. I knew there were other plainclothes guards on the floor too. And probably lots of security cameras.

"Melinda Wong," we heard Mom say. She was using her assistant-manager voice again. "I need to have a word with you."

Jasmine's aunt waved Mom away. "Can't you see I'm busy here?"

"It's urgent," Mom said.

Jasmine's aunt didn't look up from her cards right away. Maybe focus ran in the family. "I don't even know you," she said when she finally looked at Mom.

"I'm a friend of Jasmine's…"

Jasmine's aunt raised her eyebrows. "How do you know my niece?"

"She and my daughter go to the same school. To New Directions. Jasmine thinks you—" Mom dropped her voice, but we knew she was telling Jasmine's aunt about the missing money.

Jasmine's aunt wiped her eyes with the back of her hand and said something we couldn't hear. Her blond wig was coming loose at one side, and she pulled it back into place.

Mom stayed firm. "You have to come with me now. This is no place for you. Let's go now—before you go through all of your niece's savings."

Aunt Melinda had lost four hundred dollars, but we all knew it could have been worse. Of course, Jasmine was angry with her aunt. But what surprised me most was how quickly Jasmine forgave her. Her aunt was crying and going on about how sorry she was and how she hadn't been able to help herself. Her mascara left tracks on her cheeks. "All I wanted to do," she said between sobs, "was win back the money I lost."

Somehow—don't ask me how—Mom managed to talk Melinda into coming by the bank the following week. Mom wanted Melinda to meet a counselor who worked in the building next door, someone who specialized in helping people with gambling problems.

Jasmine insisted on getting a cab home with her aunt. When I turned around to look at them before we walked down to the parking garage, Jasmine's arm was around her aunt's shoulders. Aunt Melinda was adjusting her wig, which had now come halfway off. It was hard to tell who was the teenager and who was the adult.

"Hey, Mom, thanks," I said as we took the elevator down two floors to our parking spot.

"No problem. I've done that sort of thing before."

Because the elevator walls were mirrored gold, it was as if there were three more Moms and three more me's with us. "Are you saying this isn't the first time you've dragged a gambling addict away from a blackjack table?"

Mom smiled. "Not exactly. But I have spoken to a number of people with gambling addictions before and directed them to counseling. It's a fairly common problem. Anyway, I was glad to help tonight. I've been trying not to ask, but what happened to your lip anyway?"

"I sparred for the first time today." I ran the tip of my tongue over my lower lip. It still hurt, but not as much as before. "It's Jasmine's handiwork."

"I see," Mom said. Her voice didn't give anything away. "I like Jasmine. She has a big heart. But I hope you got her back."

TWENTY-FOUR

I'd never have guessed that Big Ron had contacts in the art world. But he did.

Apparently, he'd worked for years as a private bodyguard for a wealthy art collector with homes around the world, including one in Montreal.

That was how Big Ron had come to know the people who owned the Galerie Tableaux on Sherbrooke Street, near the Museum of Fine Arts. So it was Big Ron who first mentioned the street-art exhibit. A local photographer, a professor at Concordia University, had been shooting tags, graffiti and murals all over town. "Let me try to get this right," Big Ron had told Pretty Boy and me. "My friends who own the gallery say the show is a mix of street art and"—he scratched his head—"high art. Whatever the hell that means. Hopefully, not that whoever did it was getting high at the time."

"I thought you said you worked for some fancy art collector," Pretty Boy said.

Big Ron's belly shook when he laughed. "I watched his butt. I never said I picked up the lingo. Anyway, I figured you two *artistes* might want to check out the exhibit. There's what's called a *vernissage* on Thursday night. Open bar, so don't mention it to Whisky."

Even though it was a photo exhibit, I knew we wouldn't run into Cyrus—he had a low opinion of anything having to do with street art.

When we arrived at the gallery, there was already a crowd. Servers were carrying trays of champagne in fluted glasses and slivers of smoked salmon on thin spicy crackers.

Pretty Boy nudged me. "This wingding feels a little too establishment for me," he said, not bothering to lower his voice.

But when we got close enough to the walls to see the photographs, Pretty Boy stopped complaining.

There were six huge photographs of street art displayed on four walls. The photos were so sharp, so detailed, it felt as if the spray paint might drip onto the floor.

The photographer who'd shot the photos—his name was Johan Nachmann—was in the middle of the crowd, shaking hands and posing for other people's photographs.

Nachmann could have shot photos of standard tags, the kind that gave tagging a bad name—dark angular initials, sometimes even swear words—or he could have shot photos of artier tags, the kind Pretty Boy and I tried to do. Or he could have shot photos of graffiti-style murals the City had actually commissioned some street artists to do. What Nachmann did—and what made this exhibit so cool—was combine all the styles of street art, so that next to a photo of a standard tag on a dilapidated red brick building (it looked like it could have been in Montreal North) was a photo of a commissioned piece, a field of sunflowers a team of street artists had done on a wall in Notre-Dame-de-Grâce.

"I don't quite understand what Nachmann is trying to do in this exhibit," I heard a tall, elegant-looking woman wearing cat's-eye glasses say to the man with her. "Do you think he's saying that this"—she lifted her eyes, but I could tell she found it painful to look at the image of the tag on the red brick building—"is art? Because I think it's an abomination."

Pretty Boy winked at me when she said the word *abomination*.

"I don't like that particular piece of graffiti either, but I like the photo. A lot," the man said to the woman.

I couldn't resist joining the conversation. "I'm with you," I said to the man.

"Not me," Pretty Boy added. "I agree with your friend. That thing looks like a dog's breakfast. I mean, an abomination."

The woman laughed and the man shook our hands.

We checked out all six of the photos, looking at them first from a distance, then walking closer to get a different perspective. The couple moved ahead of us into a second, smaller exhibit room.

We could hear them talking before we got there. They had finally found a photo they both liked.

"Remarkable," the man said.

"Powerful, gritty," the woman added.

"Nachmann has clearly captured the work of two taggers in this photograph," the man said. "You can see that though the taggers' styles are quite different, they're working in tandem."

As soon as Pretty Boy and I walked into the smaller room, we saw the photo they were discussing. Because it had been shot at an angle, it captured two walls. One had a forest on it; the other, a larva.

The couple had stopped talking, but they were still looking at the photo, moving closer to it the way we'd been doing in the other room.

It was Pretty Boy who walked back up to them. "Just thought you might like to know—we did those tags. Me and her."

I felt the woman peering at us from behind her glasses. "Really," she said. "I'm Carole Blanchette. I teach at Concordia with Professor Nachmann. I'm doing research about street art in Montreal. I'm always interested in talking to street taggers. Let me give you my card. I'd love to interview you sometime. And this is my colleague Norman Fineberg."

The man who was with her reached out to shake our hands. "I teach studio art. If you'll allow me to be blunt, I think you two should be channeling your artistic talents in a way that doesn't involve breaking the law. You should come for a tour of our fine-arts building. I think you'd like what you see."

After giving us their business cards, Carole and Norman insisted on introducing us to Johan Nachmann and also to Antoine and Gérard, who owned the gallery.

Pretty Boy had noticed that the photograph of our work had a pretty hefty price tag. "I see you're selling that thing for five thousand big ones," he told Nachmann. "Maybe we should get a cut. After all, you couldn't have done it without us."

Nachmann stared at us and said, "There's somebody here from the *Montreal Gazette* who wants to interview me. Thank you so much for coming to the exhibit."

Antoine and Gérard were friendlier—especially after we told them we knew Big Ron.

"He worked for many years for one of our best customers," Antoine said.

"It's a shame about what happened," Gérard added, shaking his head.

Pretty Boy and I looked at each other. "What happened?" we asked at the same time.

"Big Ron didn't tell you?" Antoine said.

"He talks a lot," Pretty Boy said, which made Antoine and Gérard both laugh, "but he doesn't say much about himself."

"It's quite a story. Some gangster tried to rob his boss, the client we told you about, and Big Ron intervened," Antoine said. "We weren't there, but we heard about it afterward. Big Ron punched the robber in the head. Apparently, he hit a vein. The man was bleeding and shaking and drooling, and then he passed out cold. At first, Big Ron thought he'd killed him, but then he came to. It turned out to be a concussion—a serious one. That was the day Big Ron decided to give up the bodyguarding business."

Someone tapped my shoulder. When I saw that the person had a pencil and pad, I knew she had to be the reporter from the *Montreal Gazette*. She explained that Johan Nachmann had told her we were at the exhibit and she wanted to ask us a few questions. "I'd like to work you two into my story," she said.

She said she wouldn't use our names in her story, but she wanted to know them anyhow, and also our ages and what school we went to.

She nearly dropped her pencil when we said New Directions. "Isn't that the boxing school? The one the neighbors have been protesting about?"

"That's the one," Pretty Boy told her.

"What sort of trouble did you get in to be sent there?" she asked.

I gathered she was on deadline and needed to get straight to business. "I was expelled from my old high school for tagging. The principal had a three-strikes-you're-out rule."

Pretty Boy was cagier. "I got into my own kind of trouble" was all he said.

The reporter was scribbling away on her pad. I'd never seen such messy handwriting. I hoped she'd be able to read it when it was time to file her story.

"Hey," I said to her. "Can you put something in your story about what a great school New Directions is?" I figured we could use some good publicity.

"I'm afraid I can't say what a great school it is, because I haven't been there. But I will mention the two of you attend an alternative school. Do you believe there's some connection between the boxing and the kinds of tags you and Percy have been doing?"

I knew I had to come up with something good—and in a hurry.

"It's about change. The theme Pret—Percy and I have been exploring in our tags is change. We want people to know change is possible. Here's an example for you. Percy and I have started painting on canvas. It was for a school project, but I think we're enjoying it more than we expected to. And it's not going to get us sent to youth court. It feels like we're changing, and we're hoping people's attitudes can change too. Like the attitudes of our neighbors in Montreal North. Learning how to box has changed me."

The reporter was paying closer attention. Maybe she wanted to take boxing lessons too. "In what way?" she asked.

"I used to be afraid a lot," I told her.

"And?" she coaxed.

"Not so much anymore."

TWENTY-FIVE

Pretty Boy and I hung out at the gallery till closing time. Instead of taking the metro home, we decided to walk. The night air was warm, and walking was a way to extend what had been an amazing evening. Even Pretty Boy had to admit it was fun. "That was real champagne," he said when we were walking west on Sherbrooke Street, "not the fake kind." He'd also met Antoine's nephew. "Did you see him? He's hot. And he gave me his email. He said we should have coffee."

Sherbrooke Street is the longest street in Montreal, and it has many moods. Where the galleries are, it's got its nose in the air. It gets rougher around St-Mathieu Street, and it stays that way for a while, until it reaches Atwater Avenue and leads into Westmount, with its overpriced shops and cafés.

We were approaching St-Mathieu Street when we walked into a fight. There was no shouting, just a tension in the air like what happens before a lightning storm.

In the shadows behind a small apartment building, I spotted three guys, one much smaller than the others. The two big guys had cornered the little one. He was holding up his hands like someone surrendering in an old movie.

What was it about him that seemed familiar?

"It's that kid from next door to New Directions," Pretty Boy whispered. "What's-her-name's son."

Eddie. The gold buttons on his school blazer glinted in the dark. Why was he taking off his running shoes? Then I realized what was going on. He was being "taxed." The two bigger guys wanted Eddie's runners. I couldn't help thinking that Florence must have hemmed a lot of pants and dresses to pay for those shoes.

My eyes met Pretty Boy's. Without exchanging a word, we agreed on a plan.

We walked into the shadows. This time, I didn't freeze.

"Everything okay back there?" I called. My voice didn't shake. Not a bit. After all, I was someone to watch, wasn't I?

"Just making sure everything's cool over here," Pretty Boy added. The lightness of his tone only added to my confidence. We knew what we were doing. We were boxers. We were artists. We'd just been interviewed by the *Montreal Gazette*, hadn't we?

Eddie had already kicked off one running shoe. It was lying on its side. The kid's white athletic sock was worn at the heel. He knelt down to take off the other shoe. That's when I noticed his legs were shaking. The poor kid was terrified.

The two big guys turned toward us. I sucked in my breath when I realized one of them was the tagger Pretty Boy had beaten up in August.

He nudged his sidekick. "That's the faggot. The one who knows boxing. What the fuck are you doing here?" he asked Pretty Boy.

I didn't notice him slip his hand into his pocket. All I noticed was the flash of something silver.

He had a knife.

"Get out of here! Now!" I shouted at Eddie. But the kid didn't budge. He just stood there, shaking and pinned to the wall, one shoe off, one shoe on. I wondered afterward if it was because he was paralyzed, like I used to be around violence.

Pretty Boy's eyes were on the silver blade. I could feel him thinking. Scrambling for a plan. He'd take on the guy with the knife and leave the other one for me. The other one—the one I was going to have to take on—wasn't big. His eyes were darting back and forth between his friend and Pretty Boy in a way that made me think he was nervous. Maybe I could take him. My feet moved into fighting stance without my telling them to.

Pretty Boy didn't throw a punch. "Listen," he said, still not lifting his eyes from the blade. His voice was so calm, it was eerie. "Why don't you let this kid put his shoe back on and we'll make like none of this ever happened?"

Eddie eyed his shoe longingly.

The big guy laughed. "You afraid of a knife? Is that it, faggot?"

"I'm not afraid of a knife." How did Pretty Boy stay so calm? "And I wish you'd stop calling me faggot."

"Faggot!"

The sidekick lunged at Pretty Boy. Only later did it occur to me that I should have been insulted—he obviously hadn't thought he'd have to deal with me.

Pretty Boy was startled. Maybe that was why he didn't raise his hands to his cheeks in time. The sidekick punched Pretty Boy in the neck, and Pretty Boy yelped in pain. I nearly called out that that wasn't fair—but, of course, that would've been stupid. We were on the street. There were no rules here.

The sidekick hooted. Now it was my turn to lunge. I kicked my right leg back to gain momentum, then pushed it forward. The tip of my foot landed right where I wanted it to—in the guy's nuts.

The sidekick rolled to the ground, whimpering and cradling his crotch.

We didn't have much time.

The big guy was snorting like a horse. "What are you, some fag hag?" he asked me. Then he flicked the blade of his knife. There was laughter in his dark eyes.

Pretty Boy licked his lips. "I'm starting to think maybe you like fags more than you know." I knew Pretty Boy was trying to distract him and take his mind off me and what I'd just done to his friend.

"What the fuck do you mean by that?"

Pretty Boy's strategy worked. Only now the big guy had his knife aimed at Pretty Boy's throat.

That was when I saw something I'd never seen in Pretty Boy's eyes. Fear. Ice-cold fear.

This is it, I thought. This is where Pretty Boy's story ends. And maybe mine too. It didn't seem fair that a night that had gone so well could end up so totally wrong.

Someone whimpered. It wasn't the sidekick. He was on his knees, hunched over like he was going to puke.

It was Eddie, whimpering like a pup in a thunderstorm. Shaking too. That was when I noticed the overturned metal garbage can, its lid propped up against it, only inches from Eddie. Our eyes met and I lifted my chin just a touch, toward the lid.

The sidekick was puking. The sour stench filled my nostrils.

Eddie's eyes were bulging. I mouthed the words "Throw it!"

And he did. He picked up that dented metal lid and hurled it at the big guy. There was a clang as it made contact. The knife flew through the air, landing on the pavement with a clatter.

"What the fuck!" the big guy shouted.

Someone in an apartment on St-Mathieu Street must have phoned the police, because we heard a siren. The big guy took off, but the cops must have spotted him because when they drove up, he was in the back of the cruiser, in handcuffs.

"Not you again, Percy," one of the cops said when he saw Pretty Boy.

"He didn't do anything wrong," I said. "The guy you've got in the back of your car pulled a knife. It's over there." I'd told the others not to touch the knife—we'd left it lying on the pavement where it landed. I'd seen enough cop shows to know about fingerprints.

Eddie straightened his shoulders as he spoke to the cop. "Those two guys, Nick's the one in your car, Tommy's that one"—he gestured toward the sidekick, who was still on the ground—"wanted to steal my running shoes. Tessa and her friend"—he looked over at Pretty Boy—"tried to stop them."

"Nick and Tommy? You know them?" I asked.

"They go to my school."

"They go to St. William's?"

"Uh-huh." Eddie looked down. "They've been bullying me since I started going there. Teasing me because we live in a crappy neighborhood. They made me do bad stuff.

Stuff I shouldn't've done." His voice cracked, but he didn't cry. For a little guy, Eddie was tough. I shouldn't have been surprised. After all, he was Florence's kid.

"Hey, hey." Pretty Boy clapped Eddie on the shoulder. "We've all done some bad stuff. But just now you did good. Real good. Now, will you put your shoe back on? You're making me dizzy hopping around on one foot like that."

Pretty Boy turned to the cops. "What this little guy didn't tell you is he just saved my sorry ass."

TWENTY-SIX

Florence had organized the first town hall meeting. She also organized the second one. That was where she explained to the crowd how Pretty Boy and I had helped rescue her son from two guys who'd been bullying him ever since she'd enrolled him at St. William's School.

Eddie had never told her about the bullying—he knew how much she wanted him to succeed at the school. She even admitted she might have contributed to Eddie's stress by pressuring him to do well. Eddie had been so resentful, she explained—and I noticed how she didn't look away from the audience when she said this part—that he'd even staged a robbery at his own house. And as if that wasn't bad enough, she added, he'd shredded the sunflowers in her garden. I thought the robbery part of the story was way worse than the sunflowers, but from the way Florence told it, the flowers meant a lot to her.

Of course, she added, Eddie was getting professional help. She had also asked Big Ron to give him private boxing lessons on Saturday mornings. She even said she was considering signing up for boxing lessons herself. I was starting to think maybe Florence had a crush on Big Ron. After all, if there was one thing I'd learned since coming to New Directions it was that anything was possible.

Big Ron organized an exhibition match to mark the end of the fall term. We were going to be up against students from the West Ridge boxing team. Not only did they have high-class uniforms in their school colors, they also had a coach named Henry, who'd been on the Canadian Olympic boxing team in 1976. I think even Big Ron was intimidated.

I'd been sparring pretty regularly by that time, but always with Jasmine.

In the afternoon, after the guys had fought, I'd be up against an unfamiliar opponent. "Just keep your guard up, Tessa Blue-Rings, and do your octopus thing," Jasmine told me.

There was an emcee from the boxing federation, three judges and a scorekeeper.

Everyone had come to watch. Mom had booked the afternoon off work. Miss Lebrun had brought her little boy.

Florence and Eddie were sitting in the first row of the make-shift stands. Lady Di was next to them, Ruger by her feet, his eyes already focused on the ring. At the back, I saw the reporter from the *Montreal Gazette* who'd interviewed Pretty Boy and me.

The emcee had brought his own microphone. "In the red corner, in the fly-weight division, representing New Directions Academy and weighing one hundred fifteen point two pounds, we have Tessa Blue-Rings. This is Tessa Blue-Rings's inaugural fight." The emcee's voice bounced off the walls. "What you may not know about Tessa Blue-Rings is she's also an artist whose work you can see in photographs at Galerie Tableaux on Sherbrooke Street." Big Ron must have got the emcee to add that to my introduction.

I waved at the crowd. I hoped they couldn't tell how nervous I was.

They clapped. Someone whistled. I knew it had to be my mom or Randy. Ruger barked.

"And in this corner, hailing from West Ridge School, and weighing one hundred seventeen pounds, with a record of two wins, no losses and one knockout, we have Lydia the Lynx. Check out that boxing kimono, will you?"

Lydia the Lynx was wearing a satin kimono with a giant golden lynx silkscreened on the back. Three golden tassels hung from the sides of her boxing shoes. I knew Pretty Boy would be envious.

The audience clapped even harder for Lydia.

This was a new kind of nervous for me. Death wasn't flashing before my eyes the way it had been at the corner of St-Mathieu Street. But humiliation was. Not to mention serious pain—and, quite possibly, disfigurement.

"Settle down, Tessa Blue-Rings," Big Ron called from the corner. He must've seen how jittery I was.

The jitters slowed me down, making it harder to step away from Lydia's dance moves.

"Go get her!" a woman called from the crowd. Was that Lydia the Lynx's mom? She sounded bloodthirsty.

Lydia threw a stiff right-hand punch. I saw it coming, but I didn't get away in time and I didn't have my guard up quite right. She hit me in my temple and I fell over, wheezing. I had to get up, but I couldn't. Not yet.

I was only half aware of the ref, throwing down his hand as he counted. "One!" he shouted. Then, "Two!" He seemed to be counting in slow motion. "Three!"

I staggered to my feet. The ref looked me in the eye. I knew he was checking for blood. I gulped. I wanted to say I was fine, but the words were stuck in my throat. "Take a few steps toward me," the ref ordered, and somehow I did.

"Rotate those hips," Big Ron shouted. "Settle down!"

Only there wasn't time to settle down. Lydia was coming at me again. This time, she knocked me over again with a left hook to my jaw.

When I closed my eyes, I saw the brown spots on her lynx kimono.

The ref was counting again. "Five! Six!"

I could just lie there on the mat. Past the count of ten. What would be so terrible about that? Lydia could have a third win and second knockout on her record.

"Tessa Blue-Rings!" I heard my friends call.

I got up at the count of seven.

"Show me the Tessa Blue-Rings I know and love!" Big Ron told me just before the bell sounded for the second round.

I was tired, but I was breathing better. Maybe I'd finally started to settle down.

"Focus!" I heard Big Ron call, and I did.

Lydia extended her arm for a right hook, but I ducked. Then I came back at her with a three-punch combination. *Bam, bam, bam.* Oh, that felt good.

My muscles were loosening up. I was boxing better.

Maybe I was overconfident. Lydia knocked me down again. But this time, I was up before the count of two.

If I wanted to win, I'd have to knock Lydia out in the third and final round. Maybe, I thought, just maybe...

No one was more surprised than me when I knocked over Lydia. I looked in her eyes as she tumbled to the mat. Mostly, I saw surprise—until that moment, she hadn't taken me seriously as an opponent—but what startled me was the fear. Lydia was afraid of *me*! I nearly laughed out loud.

Looking back, I think it was the fear that made her angry. Lydia was back on her feet by the count of three, and then she came at me, pouncing, pounding, raging like a crazed lynx.

"Go get her!" the bloodthirsty woman called again.

"Go, Tessa Blue-Rings!" voices shouted.

"Protect yourself, Tessa Blue-Rings!" That was definitely my mom.

"Lydia the Lynx! Lydia the Lynx!" other voices chanted.

My arms were flailing. That was partly my strategy, but mostly that I was getting more and more tired. Focusing was harder.

"Work your combinations!" someone called. I couldn't recognize voices anymore—or even if the advice was for me or Lydia. Either way, I had to work my combinations.

Left uppercut, right uppercut. *Bam, bam.* Then a straight punch to Lydia's rib cage. I could feel my boxing glove hit flesh. Lydia fell into a heap on the mat. This time, she was up by the count of four.

She took a few more swings at me. One grazed my jaw.

Then the buzzer sounded and the round was over.

We touched gloves.

Lydia was panting. "Not bad!" she said, wiping her face with the back of her boxing glove.

"That one was yours," I told her, "but I'll be back!" I said it loud enough that my friends could hear my Schwarzenegger imitation.

The three judges handed their scores to the scorekeeper, who handed them to the emcee. I watched him unfold the pieces of paper and scan their contents.

The audience fell silent as the emcee cleared his throat. "We have," he said, "a unanimous decision. All three judges came up with the same score. Two rounds to one for Lydia the Lynx! Our winner today is Lydia the Lynx!"

I clapped as hard as anyone else. Not just for Lydia, but for me too. I'd done okay. More than okay.

Randy wanted to give me a hug. He looked insulted when I pushed him away. "Maybe later," I told him. "After I shower."

Big Ron kept pounding me on the shoulder till I finally asked him to stop.

Lydia was posing for photos with her trophy and her coach, Henry.

I was more than a little surprised when Henry said he wanted a word with me. Big Ron backed away. Afterward, I realized he probably knew what was coming.

"Blue-Rings," Henry said, pumping my hand. "I was pretty impressed by what I saw in the ring today. Terrific work in there. Great comeback. Listen, I heard your mom is here," he said, looking around for her.

My mom was just coming over to congratulate me—and inspect me for injuries. "I'm Tessa Blue-Rings's mom."

I couldn't help laughing when she said that.

Henry shook Mom's hand too. "I was just telling your daughter how well she did in there today. I'd like the opportunity to work with her. You probably know I was an Olympic contender myself." Henry's chest swelled up when he said that. "I'd like to train her, bring her along.

West Ridge offers sports scholarships, and I'm pretty sure we'll be able to offer one to Tessa"

I saw Mom's eyes brighten, her lips quiver. She was about to say something, but she decided to hold back and let me handle this.

I looked over at Pretty Boy, who was joking around with Randy and Whisky. Jasmine and Di were huddled in a way that made me think Jasmine was probably giving Di life advice. Ruger was listening too. Big Ron was showing Florence how to rotate her hips when she punched. It was the first time I'd seen Florence smile. Eddie caught my eye and gave me a thumbs-up.

"I'm totally honored," I told Henry. "I know it would be a great opportunity. But the thing is…I'm good where I am right now. Really good."

ACKNOWLEDGMENTS

I could not have written this book without the help—and inspiration—of my boxing trainer and friend, Ron Di Cecco. Thanks also to my friends the Behrendts, for introducing me to Big Ron, and to Thomas Kneubuhler and Monique Dykstra for their insights into the world of photography. As always, thanks to Viva Singer for letting me talk out yet another story. I'm also grateful to Mary Frauley and Elaine Kalman-Naves for helpful input when I needed it. Thanks to the entire team at Orca Book Publishers, especially my editor, Sarah Harvey, who, like Big Ron, pushes me to go farther than I think I can.

And, as always, thanks to my husband, Michael Shenker, and my daughter, Alicia Melamed, for being in my corner. I love you both with all my heart.

MONIQUE POLAK is the author of fifteen novels for young adults. Her historical novel *What World is Left* won the 2009 Quebec Writers' Federation Prize for Children's and Young Adult Literature. Monique has been teaching English literature, creative writing and humanities at Marianopolis College in Montreal, Quebec, since 1984. She is also an active freelance journalist whose work appears regularly in the *Montreal Gazette* and in Postmedia publications across the country. Monique is also a columnist for the ICI Radio-Canada program *Plus on est de fous, plus on lit!* Monique lives in Montreal with her husband, a newspaperman, and has a grown daughter. She has been taking boxing lessons since 2011.